PULLING LEATHER

Pickup Men, #3

L.C. CHASE

Riptide Publishing
PO Box 6652
Hillsborough, NJ 08844
www.riptidepublishing.com

Cover Art by L.C. Chase, lcchase.com/design.htm
Editor: Danielle Poiesz
Layout: L.C. Chase, lcchase.com/design.htm

ISBN: 978-1-62649-162-5

First edition
September, 2014

Also available in ebook:
ISBN: 978-1-62649-161-8

L.C. CHASE

For Mary.

TABLE OF CONTENTS

Prologue

Two years earlier . . .

Scott squeezed the steering wheel until the bones in his hands were about to bust through the skin. His jaw ached from clenching it so hard, but he couldn't leave his truck yet. He didn't want to be seen. His eyes had begun to sting from staring so intensely at the empty Ford F-150 parked near the exit of the rodeo grounds as he waited for its owner.

Most people had already cleared out, and there were only a few vehicles and equine rigs remaining. Those who wanted to revel a little longer with friends they wouldn't see again until next season. Finally, a lone form appeared from behind one of the rigs, heading his way. Through narrowed eyes, he tracked the reason he was trying—trying so hard—not to blow up and destroy everything in his path.

Tripp Colby, a man he'd been good friends with for the last three years, a fellow bull rider he'd come to think of as a brother, a man he thought he could trust, turned out to be one of *them*. A fucking *homo*. And he'd had to find out about it secondhand.

How could that be true? How could he have not known? Tripp didn't *look* gay, and he sure as hell didn't *act* gay. Nothing about the cowboy was anything short of "macho manly man." He couldn't reconcile that with being gay in his mind. Which meant it had to be a lie. A sick joke. That was the only explanation that made sense.

Except that he'd read the breaking news on the Professional Bull Riders website, when he'd bolted to the nearest internet café to confirm the hushed rumblings he'd heard all day. He'd read it in Tripp's own words, right there in flickering black and fucking white. *Gay*. No wonder Tripp had avoided him all day. Scott had never been one to hold back his opinions as to what made a man, and it sure as hell wasn't two of them doing each other.

But the ultimate betrayal came when he'd read on and learned Tripp's father had owned that fucking useless center in North Carolina. Did Tripp know Scott had been there? That they hadn't been able to fix him?

Cure the gay away, my fucking ass.

Cold sweat spread over his skin, and his pulse quickened. What if Tripp knew and had told someone?

Scott twisted his hands over the steering wheel. No, Tripp wouldn't do something like that. Not if the cowboy had been hiding.

But now, because he and Tripp had hung together for so many years, people would think he'd known about Tripp all along. That he was the same way and just trying to cover his tracks with antigay rhetoric.

Because that's what you've been doing, isn't it?

Shut up!

What if people thought the two of them were . . . involved? He shuddered, and his stomach roiled. Jesus, how many times had he thrown an arm over Tripp's shoulder like buddies did? Now people would read that differently. They'll know . . .

Tripp glanced up then, and the flash of fear that crossed his face told Scott he'd been spotted where he was sitting, parked across the road. *Fucking son of a bitch.*

The driver's door of Tripp's truck faced the road—and Scott. A box camper blocked them from view. When Tripp came around the side of his truck, looking like he was just going to get in and leave, Scott jumped from his own vehicle and stormed across the short distance between them.

"Is it true? You a cocksucking faggot?"

Tripp flinched. His shoulders dropped slightly, along with his gaze, but then he stared Scott in the eye, stuck his chin out, and rolled his shoulders back. Proud and defiant. "I'm gay, yes. We going to have a problem here?" The determination in his voice was clear. Tripp wasn't about to back down, and Scott fought a tiny flicker of unwanted admiration. No way was he going to give any props to someone like Tripp.

"Yeah, we're going to have fucking problem," Scott ground out. "You were like a brother to me, but if I'd known—"

"I haven't changed, Scott."

"The hell you haven't. What you are is disgusting. Just like my da—" Scott swallowed the word, refusing to show his shock at having almost blurted out his deepest secrets.

Tripp lifted an eyebrow. "Yesterday I was your brother, and today I'm disgusting? I'll tell you what's disgusting—" Tripp took a step closer, his fists clenching and nostrils flaring "—intolerant homophobic assholes like you who toss people out like trash because of their own fucking insecurities. People whose own lives are so fucked up they can't just let others live in peace. People who hate because of ignorance and fear and blind religion."

"You'd better step off, Tripp," Scott bit out, the words knife-edge sharp. Heat flushed through his body, and his muscles trembled with the need to hit, to hurt . . . to dominate.

"Or what?" Tripp took another step closer, close enough for Scott to see fire snapping in those ice-blue eyes, close enough to feel the turbulent charge of energy sparking between them and send a rush of blood southward. "You going to show me how much of a man you are by kicking my ass? Come on, then. Show me what you've got."

Yeah, he'd show Tripp what he had, all right. Show him that what Tripp was, that being gay, wasn't right. He grabbed Tripp by the front of his shirt with one hand and fisted the other, hauling back to deal a hard blow. But somewhere in the split second between thought and execution, wires disconnected, his groin tightened. Instead of his fist connecting with Tripp's jaw, his hand relaxed, opened, and snaked around the back of Tripp's head, yanking him forward. Their mouths and chests crashed together hard enough to force a surprised grunt from Tripp. Or from himself, he couldn't quite tell. Either way, the sound triggered the release of something primal from depths he didn't know he possessed. His only thought was to *own* Tripp. Force him to submit. He moved his lips over Tripp's in a taking that was too brutal to be called a kiss, but the need was too powerful, too consuming to fight.

A kiss.

What in the holy fuck! Scott Gillard did *not* kiss men.

And definitely did *not* get a hard-on for them.

Everything in his body seized—sharp and painful—at the horrifying realization. He shoved Tripp away so hard they both stumbled backward, but Tripp's boot heel caught on a rock, and he went down on his back with an *oof.* His chest heaved, eyes wide, mouth hanging open.

"The fuck?" The words were breathy, the shock obvious, but the sound still caused another spike of traitorous desire to pulse into Scott's groin.

Scott took another step backward, dragging the sleeve of his shirt over his mouth with enough force to abrade the skin, and then spat. He scanned the area quickly to make sure no one had seen whatever the fuck that was just happened. He could barely hear over the deafening pulse pounding like a stampede in his eardrums. The ground under his feet felt unstable, as though it was titling sideways and he'd fall off any second. "Swear to God, one word and I will make your life fucking hell. You'll wish you were never born. You get me?"

Tripp nodded, shock now replaced with confusion and something else Scott couldn't—wouldn't—identify. "Got you."

Scott stared down at Tripp, hands fisted, heart racing, and something long since dead inside him poked its head out. *Fuck.* "No," he whispered. He would never let that part of himself exist.

He turned back for his truck, his mind a confusing chaos of images and words and feelings flying by at such hyper speed he couldn't grasp a single one. In a stupor, he climbed into the cab and floored it, aware of the gravel and dust kicking up from the side of the road, but not even realizing that he'd caused it.

And then he was staring at himself in the mirror on the wall of a dingy bar bathroom he couldn't remember walking into. Hell, he couldn't even remember driving here or how much time had lapsed since he'd left Tripp on his ass in the dirt.

He studied his reflection, looking for the difference to show in some way. It didn't, but he knew it was there, lurking in the shadows like a predator, waiting for a crack in his shields so it could slip through and deal its fatal blow. He knew it was there as surely as he refused to acknowledge it.

He took his hat off, ran a hand through his hair, and met his eyes in the mirror, searching them for that thing inside that had somehow found a pinhole to slip through when he'd confronted Tripp. His gaze dropped to his mouth. Tripp flashed in his mind. *That fucking kiss.* He'd wanted to beat the shit out of Tripp, but instead he'd kissed him, and he didn't know why.

Yes, you do.

His vision clouded around the edges, closing in. Rage boiled up in his veins and exploded with his fist punching his reflection in the mouth. Glass shattered into an intricate spiderweb, shards fell into the sink below, and red streaks stained the fragments.

Nothing changed.

Pain didn't register. Release did not come. Answers remained staunchly elusive. Anger still bubbled in his blood, but a growing sense of defeat held it below the surface. This fight had been going on too long for him to *not once* gain the upper hand. He'd only managed to ignore it, hold the inevitable at bay, but he'd never been able to eradicate it. And now . . . now he was just exhausted from a lifetime of fighting a losing battle.

He looked down at his hand, flexed and curled his fingers, but felt nothing. Mindlessly, he turned on the water, watching the blood on his knuckles dilute from red to pink to clear. The water may have been cold or may have been hot, but he couldn't tell which. If he weren't seeing it sluice over his skin, he wouldn't have known it was running at all. He turned off the tap, pulled enough paper towels from the dispenser to wrap his hand in a makeshift bandage, and then went back out to the bar without looking up at the mirror again.

"Black and tan," he told the bartender when he sat back down at his stool. The bartender eyed him for a second, then nodded and silently went about filling Scott's order. *Now would be a good time for a cigarette, if I smoked.* Scott's phone buzzed in the back pocket of his jeans. There wasn't a single person on the planet he wanted to talk to right now. Retrieving the phone, he turned it off without looking at the caller ID, and then tossed it facedown on the bar.

"Looks like you could use a little something extra," the bartender said, placing a tequila shooter, a lemon slice, and saltshaker on the bar beside the beer.

"Yeah. Thanks." Scott pulled a couple of bills from his wallet and placed them on the bar top, but the bartender handed them back.

"This round's on the house, man."

"Thank you," Scott said but pushed the money back toward the man and added a few more bills. "For the bathroom mirror."

The bartender nodded. "Fair enough." He scooped up the cash and then left Scott to his drink and his thoughts.

He tried to pick up the glass with his bandaged hand, but a sharp stab of pain had him pulling back. Why the fuck didn't he beat the shit out of Tripp instead of a goddamned mirror? That's what the lying cocksucking asshole deserved. Just like what his father had deserved for leaving Scott and his mom to wallow in poverty—for another man. But he hadn't dealt that blow, either.

Because you're the same.

No! I am not *like them!*

He shot back the tequila with his good hand—the bartender had given him the top-shelf stuff—and held the glass up for a refill.

The barkeep was about the same height as Tripp, and his hair was longer but just as jet black. His eyes were brown rather than blue, but the resemblance was enough to spark a visual recall of his earlier confrontation with Tripp. Except this time, he was wrapping his arms around Tripp, pulling him closer, kissing him . . . his hands in Tripp's hair . . . hips rocking together . . .

And why was he still thinking about that fucking kiss? Thinking about what would have happened if Tripp had reciprocated?

You know why.

"Fuck." Could that stupid voice in the back of his head not shut the fuck up?

Scott squeezed his eyes shut, dropped his head into his uninjured hand, and a near sob escaped his mouth. *I don't want this.*

"There you are, you son of a bitch," Billy hollered. He crossed the bar to where Scott sat and pulled up the stool beside him, while Kevin stumbled into the stool on Scott's other side. Fellow bull riders and cohorts, they'd shared more experiences than he could remember, from rodeo to women to getting drunk and bar brawling. Friends or not, they were the last people he wanted to deal with right now.

"We've been trying to get a hold of you, asshole," Kevin said. "Why aren't you answering your phone?"

Scott frowned and picked up the phone. He couldn't remember turning it off, but the screen was black. He turned it back on and quick scroll through recent calls showed he'd missed seven calls from the two of them.

"Didn't notice," he said, his voice flat and completely devoid of emotion. He also hadn't noticed almost three hours had passed since his confrontation with Tripp.

"You missed out," Kevin said and grinned.

"Round of Jack here." Billy smacked his hand on the bar surface, earning a quick scowl from the bartender. Then Billy elbowed Scott in the ribs and leaned in slightly. "We got him, man."

A tickle of unease lifted the hairs on the back his neck. "Got who?"

"That faggot, Colby," Kevin jumped in. The bile rose up the back of Scott's throat.

"Yeah," Billy said. "We saw him drivin' and followed him till he stopped for gas—"

"Then we took him out back and taught him what a real man is," Kevin finished, a note of pride in his voice. "We tried calling you 'cause we knew you wouldn't want to miss out."

"Fuck, you should'a seen it." Billy beamed, and Scott's stomach flipped. Yes, he was pissed—furious, even—and he'd wanted to kick the shit out of Tripp too, had found him to do just that, but when it came to it, he hadn't been able to. Tripp had been a good friend to him over the years. He liked Tripp. Not *like* like, but . . . Maybe he always knew Tripp was hiding something. Maybe he felt a connection with Tripp he couldn't quite define—or didn't want to—but instinctively knew was there. He still couldn't line up all the pieces in a way that made sense to him, but at the end of the day, if he'd wanted Tripp hurt, he'd have done it himself.

Scott stared hard at the drink in front of him and forced his voice to remain unaffected. "How'd you leave him?"

"Who cares?" Kevin said.

"Yeah, one less freak in the world," Billy added.

Red clouded Scott's vision, and he clenched his jaw tight, fighting back the urge to drill both these assholes into the ground. No matter how angry he was, no matter how much he hated his dad for destroying their family, and now Tripp for being one of them too, he didn't wish them dead. His stomach churned, and his throat tightened at the sickening realization: it was his fault. If he'd answered his phone, he may have been able to prevent Billy and Kevin from doing anything.

And why the fuck did he care so much?

Because you're the same.

The bartender lined up three shot glasses on the table in front of them, and the look he gave Scott drove the nail of unexpected guilt a little deeper into his gut. He pushed back and stood abruptly.

"Gotta go." He pocketed his wallet and phone, diligently avoiding eye contact with anyone.

"What? Dude, what about shots?" Billy said.

"Yeah, man." Kevin chimed in. "We gotta celebrate."

Scott shook his head, still not making eye contact. "I, uh . . . got a date."

He bolted from the bar before they could say anything more. His heart pounded hard in his chest and loud in his ears, and a sense of urgency had him running for his truck while grabbing his phone and pressing Tripp's number at the same time.

"C'mon, c'mon," he chanted as he hopped into the truck and cranked the ignition, but the call went to voice mail. He pulled out onto the road, guessing at which direction Tripp would have gone. It wasn't like he could go back into the bar and ask the guys for details without arousing suspicions.

He drove for what felt like hours, but was probably only half of one, when he finally spotted Tripp's truck at a travel station. Pulling around to the back of the building where the guys had said they'd hauled Tripp, he didn't see anything at first. But there, against the wall and half behind the dumpster, was a lifeless body lying in an awkward huddle.

"Jesus Christ." Scott slammed the truck into park and ran to Tripp, dropping down at his side. His face was swollen, bruised, and bloody, his left leg at an unnatural angle, and who knew what other damage he'd suffered internally. Scott felt for a pulse, and cold sweat broke out across his skin when he couldn't find one. But then a faint bump against his fingertips sent a rush of relief through him. Tripp was alive, but barely. And he'd stay that way if Scott could get him to help fast enough.

He ran to his truck, backing it up as close to Tripp as he could get, and then gathered all the blankets and jackets he had from the back of the cab. He dropped the tailgate and threw everything onto the floor of the box.

Very carefully, he gathered Tripp in his arms and carried him to his truck, placing him on the makeshift bed. He bunched up the sides to help keep Tripp from moving too much while he drove.

"Hang on, Tripp."

Half an hour later, Scott was pulling out of the emergency parking lot. He hadn't gone inside, hadn't given anyone any info, just shouted from the doorway that a man needed help. Nurses and attendees had responded quickly, and while they were busy attending to Tripp, Scott had taken off.

Not even three blocks from the hospital, he had to pull over at the side of the road. He dropped his head to the steering wheel and closed his eyes. He couldn't take much more of this day. Hopefully Tripp would be okay. That he himself would be okay was doubtful. Not after that kiss and the realization that this constant, exhausting fight against his true self was futile. "Fuck. Fuck-fuck-fuck."

Chapter One

"You can do this, hon." Brandi leaned across the cab of his truck and squeezed his thigh. The gesture was supportive, encouraging, and he needed it more than he'd ever admit. She smiled before sitting back in the passenger seat. "Take as long as you need. I'll be right here."

Not for the first time, he wondered why he couldn't have fallen for Brandi Saunders. She was perfect, the one person who truly knew him—and all of his secrets—and still stood by him. People had thought she was a regular girl he visited on the tour, a favorite buckle bunny, but she was never a *regular* girl. It had served him well to let people think they were more, and they had crossed that line once early in their friendship but realized pretty quickly that wasn't a road they were meant to follow. The reality was, and always had been, that they were more like brother and sister.

"Thank you, Bran." He forced a smile he wasn't feeling. "I don't know what I'd have done if you hadn't been there for me." Following the incident two years ago, he'd slid into a tailspin. After the big-ass cherry on his wake-up call—being arrested on suspicion for Tripp's assault—he'd reached out to her for help. He'd refused to see a therapist, but as a clinical social worker for a nonprofit mental health center, she had the skills to guide him through his haze of confusion and self-hate and bring him back to life—his true life.

"Good thing you have me then, isn't it?" She gestured toward the ranch house they'd parked in front of. "Now go."

Easier said than done. He turned back to the house that Tripp Colby shared with Marty Fairgrave. He knew it was an important part of his recovery process, but fuck. Now that he was here, how was he supposed to look Tripp in the eye, knowing he could have changed the course of that night? Or face Marty, with all the shitty things he'd said to the man over the years?

"Stop." Brandi reached across the console and cupped his chin, turning him to face her. "I see what's going on in your head. You need to do this and you *can* do this. Okay?"

He nodded, then covered her hand with his and pulled it to his lips to kiss her palm. He hated feeling so off-kilter, but she gave him a kind of strength he'd never known he needed.

Which promptly about-faced when he looked back at the house to see Marty standing on the edge of the front steps, foreboding and unwelcoming. Scott sucked in a deep breath and held it for a three-beat before slowly releasing. This had to be done. Whatever Marty and Tripp had to dish out, he was more than willing to accept. Wasn't like he deserved a second chance, or would be forgiven, but he had to make the effort. If for nothing else than his own peace of mind.

He turned to Brandi. "I couldn't do this without you."

"Yes, you could. Eventually." She gave his hand a gentle squeeze, then let go and pulled an e-reader from her bag on the floor. "Now go. I have a love story to finish reading while you're doing your thing. They're just about to have sex."

He groaned and rolled his eyes. He really did love her.

He carefully placed his cowboy hat on his head, and then with another deep breath, opened the door and stepped out into a warm California afternoon. He fought the urge to fidget, stick his hands in his pockets, pull his hat down to cover his eyes . . . or turn tail and run back home as fast as possible.

Marty's expression didn't change, but a hint of curiosity churned in the depths of unusually hard, flinty eyes.

Scott stopped a few feet from the bottom of the steps, and the front door swung open. His breath caught in the back of his throat when Tripp stepped out . . . using a cane.

After his meltdown following that night, Scott had disappeared from the rodeo world completely, but he'd looked up all he could find on Tripp once he'd finally come to accept who he was. He knew the injuries Tripp had suffered had cost him his career as a professional bull rider, but to actually see it . . . If Scott had been paying attention, if he'd truly been a *real* man then, he could have prevented the severity of it—or maybe all of it. And no, the irony in that was not lost on him.

Tripp stopped beside Marty, and Marty slipped his arm around Tripp's waist, defiance and warning on both their faces.

"What are you doing here?" Tripp said, his voice hard and tight.

Scott lowered his gaze to the base of the bottom step and then looked up at the couple on the porch: at Tripp who had been like a brother, at Marty, one of the best pickup men on the circuit who'd once saved Scott's life at a rodeo, even though he was an asshole. They were good men, strong men, and neither had deserved any of the shit he'd dished out over the years.

He shouldn't be here.

He glanced over his shoulder to find Brandi not reading as she'd said she would but watching him. She nodded her head, giving silent support. Scott took another deep breath, turned back to the cowboys whose feet he bowed at, and removed his hat.

"I . . . uh . . ." He cleared his throat, swallowed hard, and looked Tripp in the eyes. "I came to apologize to you. For that night. For what happened and what it cost you. I just wanted you to know I'm real sorry about that. If I could, I'd go back and change things so it never would have happened. And . . ." He slid his gaze to Marty. "I also wanted to apologize for being a first-class homophobic asshole to you for so long."

The way both men stood so still, staring at him like they could skin him in three seconds flat, made him want to squirm, to run. He shifted the hat in his hands and dropped his gaze. "I don't expect forgiveness or nothing, and I'm not asking for it. I just wanted to come here in person and tell you how sorry I am for everything, and if I can help it, I won't let something like that happen to anyone else."

A horse whinnied in the distance, a bee buzzed past his face, and the silence stretched. He flicked his eyes up quickly. The couple didn't look like they were going to tear him apart anymore, but now their expressions were blank.

"Okay. Well. I'll be on my way then."

"What happened?" Tripp stepped forward as Scott was about to turn away. "You disappeared for two years and now here you are, apologizing on my doorstep."

"You guys remember Brandi?" He waved his hat in the direction of the truck. "She helped me come to terms with a few things about myself. See the error of my ways, so to speak. Now I'm trying to be a better person, live a truer life, and make amends for all the grief I've caused others."

"You were a hard-core asshole, Scott," Marty said. His voice was stony, but his expression had softened. "How can we believe you're for real here?"

Scott stared him dead in the eyes. "Would the old Scott be on your doorstep of his own accord, offering apologies?"

A small smile tipped up one side of Marty's mouth. "Point taken."

Silence fell between them again, thick and weighty.

"Well. That was all I really had to say. So . . ." Scott glanced out at the land Tripp and Marty shared—Marty's family ranch in Bridgeport was an impressive spread—but he didn't really see it. "I'll just be on my way then."

Tripp and Marty nodded, and Scott turned to leave. A bead of sweat trickled down the side of his face. Why did the truck feel like he'd parked it twenty miles away rather than twenty feet? The longer he walked, the farther away it seemed. Emotions he couldn't pin bounced around inside his chest: relief that he'd said his piece, disappointment that he hadn't been forgiven, jealousy at the easy way they stood together, loneliness at the nothing he had in his life to look forward to.

"Scott," Tripp called just as he'd reached the truck. He stopped, fighting down a rise of hope. He knew he deserved nothing less than hatred, apathy at the very least, but deep down, he couldn't deny he'd hoped for at least a hint of forgiveness. "Why don't you come and work with me on the gay rodeo circuit?"

Scott blinked. *Gay* rodeo? Him? That was . . . He didn't know. His brain stalled out, and an odd panic nudged at his senses.

Marty snapped his gaze to Tripp, eyebrows raised. "What?"

Tripp placed a hand on Marty's hip. "Trust me, okay? I think it will be good for him."

Marty's pose, the expression on his face, his eyes, everything softened when he looked down at Tripp, and then he smiled, and a little spike of jealousy poked its head out. Shit, what was wrong with him? Self-acceptance was still a struggle sometimes, and he was a long way from wanting anything like what Tripp and Marty had—just seeing two guys together still made him uncomfortable. So why the touch of green now?

Tripp turned back to Scott, his voice kind and smile welcoming. "They don't have as many events as the pro tour, and a lot are out of state, so I work with them, and the PBR on off weeks. What do you say?"

Scott swallowed. "But . . . I haven't even been on a bull in two years."

"Not to ride. To work with me. I teach bull riding at the rodeo schools on both tours, and I also work with the PBR to promote awareness and acceptance for all cowboys, regardless of orientation. I think it would be good for you to spend some time in the boots of those you've been spitting on for so many years. Maybe also help make others think before they spit."

Scott had to admit the idea of getting back to the rodeo appealed, but to work with a bunch of gay men? Him? They'd probably string him up and quarter him the first day. Just for kicks. "Thank you, Tripp, but I'm not sure that would be a good idea. I have a feeling the old Scott is all people are going to see."

"Which is more reason to show them this new one, isn't it? That if a hard-ass prick like you can turn it around . . .?"

"He makes a great point." Scott started at Brandi's voice right beside him. He hadn't realized she'd left the truck and joined them. He glanced over at her, and she smiled back. The glint in her soft blues eyes told him he'd better accept the offer if he knew what was good for him. And he did. A mad Brandi was the last thing he wanted to deal with, but this might be a bigger step than he was ready for.

Scott looked back at Tripp. "Thank you, but I'll need to think on it."

"Please do," Tripp said.

CHAPTER TWO

"You okay?" Brandi asked as they bounced down the long drive from the Fairgrave Ranch, dust lifting into the sky in their wake.

Scott thought for a moment, taking stock of the last half hour. "Yes, I think I am." And he wasn't just giving her lip service. He felt lighter somehow, having taken a much-needed step forward and been offered an olive branch. That was so much more than he could have ever hoped for, and was far more than he deserved. That Tripp would extend an offer like that to him only proved how much bigger a man Tripp was, and had always been. It had been a humbling moment, and even if he never accepted the offer, he would always be grateful for that quick acceptance.

"You should honestly give it some thought," she said. "About joining Tripp."

"Do you really think that's such a good idea?" Scott slowed to a stop at the end of the drive before turning onto the gravel road and starting the long trip back to Cupertino. "I can't imagine too many people there would be all that excited about having me around."

He couldn't deny how much the idea appealed. He'd missed the rodeo circuit and deep down would love to get back on it, but people would remember and expect the old Scott. He wasn't that person anymore—most of the time, anyway. Would they even accept who he was now? The real Scott Gillard? He doubted it, especially after the way he'd treated people for so long, letting his own internalized hate and anger bleed out to everyone around him. If the boot were on the other foot, he'd just as soon not have anything to do with himself, either. No matter how much he may have changed.

"Maybe you should try giving people the benefit of the doubt," she said. "They might surprise you."

Scott shook his head. "No. The cowboys on the gay circuit will hate me for being the homophobic prick I was, and the cowboys on the straight circuit will hate me either for being . . ." He swallowed and glanced out his side window at the passing landscape. "You know . . . *that way* now. Or for what I did to Billy and Kevin. It's a no-win situation."

"People will react how they'll react. You can only control how you respond to them," she said. Her voice had taken on that warm, supportive professional tone she used when she slipped into therapist mode. "And you did the right thing by turning in Billy and Kevin. Anyone with half a brain can see that."

"I doubt Dex will ever see it that way," he said. With the added charge of a hate crime on top of their assault, and the loss of Tripp's career due to the attack, Billy and Kevin were still in prison and would likely be there for a few more years. Dex, Billy's younger brother, had been none too pleased.

"Again, you can only control your own actions and reactions."

"How am I supposed to react when they start calling me the same things I'd called others? Or if they decide the world would be better off without the likes of me in it?"

"You know how, hon." Her voice softened—therapist out, best friend in. "We've been working on that for months now. You have a solid handle on your anger, you know how and when to walk away, and you can defuse a situation before it escalates."

Could he? Yes, they'd spent a lot of time working through his anger issues and strategies to manage it. He did feel he had a pretty good grip on it, wasn't as fast to anger as he used to be, but then, he'd been keeping a pretty low profile since his meltdown, and away from situations where he'd lost it in the past. He'd even rented his ranch, leased out his horses, and moved into Brandi's house. It had been her request, but he'd never told her how grateful he'd been for the offer. Living alone, with his chaotic thoughts and dark memories, was driving him over the edge. He'd stopped eating, started drinking, and more than once eyed the shotgun locked in a glass cabinet in his den. He didn't know if he'd have pulled himself out of the fugue on his own, or actually opened that gun cabinet, but Brandi had saved him from ever finding out.

The worst of it was behind him now, and he probably should have moved out a year ago, especially since he had a perfectly good house of his own in Stockton, but he hadn't felt ready to be on his own yet. The plan had been that he'd stay there for a few months while he got himself sorted, but it turned out sixteen years' worth of anger and dangerous, destructive thinking took a fair bit longer to correct.

"I know how much you miss it," Brandi said, her voice softer. "Rodeoing, bull riding, traveling. That's who you are. Everything else is secondary, and that's what you need to learn and for people to see. You could be a positive role model for someone."

Scott barked out a strangled laugh. "I'm an asshole!"

"*Were*. Show 'em who you are now, because I know that guy, and believe it or not, he's kind of likeable."

He had a chance to get back into the scene, and hell, he needed that, but a role model? Unlikely. Maybe she and Tripp were right and this could be a good thing, though, for him to show he'd learned his lessons and was making amends. If he could, then others could too.

Scott sighed and turned to meet her sky-colored eyes. Never having been able to hide what he was thinking from her, Brandi smiled and lifted his phone out of the center console, giving it a waggle. "Call Tripp."

CHAPTER THREE

"What the hell are you doing here?"

Scott sighed. Not even clear of the parking area at the Morgan Hill grounds—the site of his first-ever gay rodeo, though today was the schooling that preceded rodeo weekend—and already someone recognized him as the homophobic asshole he used to be. He slanted a quick glance in the direction of the voice. He didn't recognize the three cowboys behind him, nor did he know which one had spoken, but it didn't matter. That was exactly the reception he'd expected, and he was beginning to wonder the same thing. What *was* he doing here? He'd agreed with Tripp and Brandi that it could be good for him, but it sure didn't seem so good for anyone else right now. Why on earth would anyone accept his ass there?

"It's okay, Davey," Tripp said. He'd been waiting by his truck when Scott arrived, and now stood at Scott's shoulder in a show of support. "He's here to work with me, not to make trouble."

Davey's eyebrows disappeared under the brim of his cream-colored cowboy hat, and he turned to his two buddies in surprise. All three looked back at Tripp like he'd grown a third head.

"After what he did to you? How can that be okay?" Davey puffed out his chest, which, because his shirt was unbuttoned to about midchest, effectively drew attention to thick, hair-covered pectorals and the tail end of a tattoo over one. Scott quickly averted his eyes. Fortunately, the men seemed too stunned by Tripp's comment to have noticed what he'd been looking at.

Tripp shrugged. "Just is. There are two sides to every story, and everyone deserves a second chance."

"And some dogs just need to be put down," said the man wearing a ball cap and Gym Bear tank top to Davey's right. Then he sneered at Scott, spit a chunk of tobacco out of the side of his mouth, and walked away. Davey and the third cowboy—who wasn't wearing a shirt at all, leaving his tattoos and muscles on full display—gave Scott a disdainful perusal that said he'd been judged and found wanting.

Davey, who was about Scott's height and size, took a step forward, and Scott met his gaze without challenge. All he could see there was distrust and contempt.

"You just stay clear of me, you hear?"

Scott nodded, dropped his eyes, and dug his hands into his pockets, fighting back the sudden urge to knock that look right off Davey's face. But that was the old Scott. The one he'd been trying so hard to purge these past two years. It was getting easier, but this was the first time someone had gotten up in his face like that since, and it triggered an instinct he was still struggling to manage.

Scott heard their boot heels on the hard dirt fade as they walked away, but he didn't look.

"They'll come around eventually," Tripp said, and Scott froze for a second when Tripp reached out and squeezed his shoulder. He swallowed back the old reactions that the minor confrontation with Davey had brought to the surface. Not having noticed, or ignoring it if he had, Tripp tipped his head toward the livestock pens. "C'mon, you're going to help me teach some greenhorns how to rope and ride."

Scott nodded and fell into step beside him. "Why are you doing this for me?"

Tripp stopped and turned to look him in the eyes, searching them briefly. "I know you're the one who got me to the hospital that night. Took a while, but I remembered hearing your voice telling me to hold on. If you hadn't done that, I don't think I'd be standing here right now."

Scott shifted his gaze over Tripp's shoulder to stare unfocused at the trees lining the rodeo grounds. "You'd still be riding bulls if I'd got there sooner."

Tripp shook his head. "You can't know that. You know as well as I do that every ride could be our last. But it's neither here nor there. This is where we are now. Okay?"

Scott nodded, but it wasn't okay. If he hadn't turned the ringer off and answered his phone that night, things would have ended differently, and Tripp would still be competing. Maybe Scott would be too.

"Besides, I know a thing or two about having to live your life hiding who you are. Granted, I didn't go to the extremes you did, but . . . I have to make a confession." Now Tripp was the one looking away. He swallowed and then said, "I kind of used our friendship as a decoy. In the beginning. A sheep in wolf's clothing, if you will."

Scott huffed out a mirthless laugh. "So the added bonus of hanging out with the biggest homophobe on the circuit was that no one would ever question you."

"Something like that, yeah." Tripp grimaced.

"Huh," Scott said, making sure to keep his voice monotone. "Guess we both had them fooled."

Tripp stared at him for a long second, and then one side of his mouth lifted to form a crooked grin.

Scott couldn't help grin back, and in the brief moment that their eyes met and people and animals moved around them in the background, something passed between them. An understanding, a camaraderie Scott had never felt before because this time, it was coming from a place of pure honesty. This time, he was meeting another as his true self. He maybe couldn't say it out loud—he hadn't moved beyond the abstract and attempted to experience what that meant—but the fact that he wasn't constantly fighting himself, and by extension the whole world, was a huge step in the right direction. And having Tripp stand there beside him, without judgment, without condition, meant more than he would ever be able to voice.

"What happened that night . . ." The saliva in Scott's mouth was suddenly too thick to swallow, and he couldn't get the rest of his words out. He motioned between them.

Tripp shook his head. "That's yours to tell, if you ever want to."

Scott nodded. Took three attempts to clear his throat. "Thank you."

"C'mon." Tripp resumed their walk toward the corrals. "I'll introduce you to a few of the guys later. For now, work's awaiting."

Scott glanced around, and his gaze landed on four men near the chutes watching him with varying degrees of curiosity, indifference, and hostility. Three were sitting on the railing, one holding the reins to a horse, but the fourth man was sitting astride a bay quarter horse. That last one sent a little thrill racing up Scott's spine and a flush of heat over his skin. The cowboy looked young, early twenties at most, and the way his hat shaded his face highlighted well-defined cheekbones and a slight pout to his mouth. He wore a red shirt that matched the reins-holding cowboy—which meant the two were probably pickup men—and a silver conch-covered belt matched the band around his hat.

Scott quickly looked away, forcing down the heat, and followed Tripp. He wasn't ready to acknowledge what that rush meant, and he sure as hell wasn't ready to act on it. Not when a distant urge to fight it still lingered.

Cory watched Tripp and a cowboy he'd never seen before disappear behind the chutes. He'd noticed them the moment they'd come around the concession from the parking lot and passed by the arena. Well, not *them*, exactly, but the new cowboy. He was a couple of inches shorter than Tripp's six feet, and a whole lot buffer—broad shoulders, big chest, solid thighs. Dark hair peeked out from under a black hat, day-old scruff peppering the strong jawline of a pretty-in-a-really-rugged-way face. *Dayum*. The set of the cowboy's shoulders, down and slightly rolled in, seemed at odds with his natural stature. He should be walking tall and commanding with a body like that, but instead seemed insecure, wary.

Cory turned in the saddle to the three men sitting on the fence by the chutes—his overprotective brother Toby, his fellow pickup man Harlan, and Harlan's boyfriend, Ben. "Who is that hot-as-sin cowboy?"

"Can't be, but sure as hell looks like Scott Gillard. Biggest fucking homophobe on the pro tour," Harlan said, a hint of snarl evident in his voice. Cory frowned. Harlan might be a tough-looking kick-ass cowboy, but he was one of the biggest teddy bears Cory had ever met. He would never in his life have imagined Harlan could sound so hard.

"Scott? Here?" Ben's eyebrows shot up, and he whistled. "Heard he took a crowbar to Tripp's leg."

Harlan shook his head. "No, I heard he sent his buddies in to do the dirty work."

"Left him for dead is what they all did," Ben countered. "Would be too, if someone hadn't happened along and got Tripp to the hospital in time."

Cory leaned back in his saddle, eyes bouncing back and forth between the two. "You two sound like a couple of gossiping hens. Anyone know what really happened?"

They glanced at each other, shrugged, and then turned back to Cory. "All we know for sure," Harlan said, "is Scott and Tripp were friends until Tripp came out. Next thing we hear, Tripp's been bashed so bad he won't ever compete again and Scott's been arrested."

"Was he convicted? Did he go to jail?"

Ben shrugged again, swatting at a fly. "Dunno. Didn't hear anything after that and then he just disappeared. Until now."

"Rolled on his friends to avoid doin' time, I heard." Harlan looked over to where Tripp and Scott had disappeared into the livestock pens behind the arena. "And we don't need his kind of hate here."

"Definitely someone you need to steer clear of," Toby said, his voice hard with the warning. Cory glared at him. He loved how his older brother had watched out for him when they were growing up, but at twenty-four years old, he was a full-grown adult who could take care after himself just fine now, thank you very much. Could even pull up his big-boy pants all by himself.

"If he was so bad, why is he here with Tripp?" Cory earned an evil eye from Toby and a headshake from Ben.

"That's what I'd like to know," Harlan said.

Cory would reserve judgment until he met the man in person. And he fully intended to do that the first chance he got. Having been constantly subject to judgment himself simply because of his appearance or mannerisms, he wasn't about to do the same to anyone else. Just because Cory was smaller than most cowboys, or was too femme with his silk shirts, rhinestones, and makeup for the more butch guys, didn't mean he couldn't handle pickup. He'd proved time and again he could, eyeliner and all, and could do it better than most. Plus, if Tripp had been able to forgive whatever it was Scott had supposedly done, who was he to not give the guy a chance too?

Banging against the rails drew the attention of all four men. Tripp and Scott were pushing a few steers through the narrow chute toward the roping stalls. Well, Scott was pushing them, but Tripp was using the rails for support and nudging them along with his cane. The morning sun's rays speared through kicked-up dust that swirled around Scott's legs, silhouetting his lower body against an ethereal glow. Something about that image burned into Cory's mind and made his mouth water.

Scott looked up, and their gazes collided for a split second, Scott's eyes full of hunger. It may as well have been electrically charged with the way Cory's heart stalled out a beat from the punch of it. Scott pursed his lips and broke the connection, turning back to his task.

"Is he gay?" Cory asked no one in particular, still watching Scott work.

"Scott Gillard?" Incredulity kicked the pitch of Harlan's voice up a notch. "You're kidding, right? No way, no how is that man gay."

"Huh." Cory wasn't so sure. Not after that look they'd just shared and still feeling the effects of it.

"Hey, Cory," Tripp called. "You want to help with hazing?"

He had to take a breath and give himself a mental shake after the jolt meeting eyes with Scott had given him. "You mean like actually running guide for the steer wrestlers or just herding the steers out when they're done? 'Cause I can do both."

"*Cory . . .*" Toby said, his voice low but firm. Cory slanted a *back off* glare at him before reining his horse toward Tripp and the hunky I-want-but-maybe-should-stay-away-from Scott.

"Probably just herding them out, but I'm sure there'll be one or two greenhorns with no bulldogging partners."

Cory smiled. "On it."

Harlan, who sometimes acted like another older brother—but the cool kind who didn't rat him out when he got up to stupid stuff—tapped Toby's shoulder before jumping down off the fence. "I'll help too," he said as he mounted up, earning a glare from Toby.

"Thanks, guys," Tripp said when they rode over to the roping chutes. He tipped his head in Scott's direction. "This is Scott, a friend of mine." Then to Scott said, "Cory Ackerson and Harlan Bennett. Pickup men."

Cory leaned down in his saddle and stuck his hand out, earning a startled look from Scott. He smiled his best, flirtiest smile. "Nice to meet you."

Scott hesitated, like he wasn't sure if he should accept the gesture or if it was even real. He shot a quick sideways look at Tripp, and his brows dipped a notch, nonplussed. He took a step forward and accepted the shake. Scott's hand engulfed his, and the grip was firm . . . and much too fleeting. "Nice meetin' you too."

His voice was a low, gravelly rumble that sent a shiver skipping across the surface of Cory's skin. Dark eyes met his briefly before dropping away as if embarrassed or unsure. The dichotomy of a man who looked like someone people in a crowded room would step aside for, and yet seemed as if he'd rather hide behind Tripp and not be noticed at all, intrigued Cory. Whatever Scott's story was, he wanted to hear it.

Scott turned his focus to Harlan and this time offered a handshake first.

Harlan scowled. "I know who you are." His voice was flat and cutting. Scott nodded, dropped his hand, and stepped back, to the side of but slightly behind Tripp. His hand twitched, like maybe he was fighting not shoving it in his pocket. Or making a fist.

Cory glared at Harlan and mouthed, *Bitch*, but Harlan only returned the look with a shrug. Cory didn't know the story behind Tripp's injuries, or anything about Scott other than what the gossip queens had shared. He didn't know if he should be so receptive about Scott being there, but something about the way Scott held himself inward, broken, called out to Cory. He had the sudden urge to hop down off his horse and give the cowboy a hug.

"You just here helping out for the weekend, Scott, or you going to be a regular?"

Scott jerked, as if he'd been surprised at being addressed, and his wide eyes met Cory's again. "I . . . uh . . ." He shifted on his feet, and this time he did shove his hands in his pockets. "Just the weekend for now, I guess. See how it goes."

"Cool." Cory smiled. One side of Scott's mouth rose a touch, like he was about to smile in response but refused to let it loose. He nodded once and then turned back to getting the steers sorted.

Cory glanced over at Tripp and raised an eyebrow, but Tripp shook his head. No matter, he'd pin him down later and get the whole story.

Chapter FOUR

Scott sat down at a table in the shade and bit into his hamburger. It had been a long morning, and muscles he hadn't used in ages ached, but it felt damn good to be back in the rodeo environment. It was a little different than the one he used to compete in, but everything that mattered was the same—the sounds and smells of livestock, the excitement of the events, the camaraderie of the cowboys. Even though that last bit didn't include him. He was definitely wearing someone else's boots now. The shunner had become the shunee.

He looked down at his plate. Was this what he'd done to Marty and the others all those years? Made them feel this unwanted, this disdained, this . . . less than? And why? Just because they were . . . that way? Like him. His stomach roiled, and his lunch made a halfhearted backward lurch. What he couldn't identify anymore was if that lurch was because he hated who he was or because of what he'd done to others on account of that hate?

So far, aside from Tripp and the young pickup man, Cory, no one had willingly spoken to him. Fortunately, no one had been as unwelcoming as Davey, the openly hostile cowboy he'd met when he first arrived on the rodeo grounds that morning, but there was definitely some animosity coming off a few others in heavy waves. Scott might be walking in Marty's boots right now, but he rightfully earned and deserved what he was getting. Marty never did. None of those other men he'd belittled did, either. They had done nothing other than be themselves, embrace who they were, and stand tall, and what had he done? Resented them for it, hated himself for it, and cut every one of them down because of it.

He dropped his unfinished burger on the plate and pushed it away, appetite gone. *Fuck, I'm such an asshole.*

The table shook, and Scott looked up into a pair of flinty gray eyes. *Great. Perfect timing.*

Davey sat across from him, flanked by the other two less-than-thrilled cowboys who'd been with Davey, earlier. The two looked like a couple of mafia goons, with their matching scowls and arms folded across chests deliberately pushed out. Only, as buff as they were, they really weren't all that intimidating. In the past, Scott would have chewed these guys up and spit them out like they were nothing. But that was the old Scott. The hate-myself-angry-at-the-world Scott, and he didn't want to be that person again. That person was exhausting.

"You've got a lot of balls, coming here," Davey said, a bitter edge to his voice. "What makes you think anyone wants you around?"

Scott clenched his jaw. He knew things like this were bound to happen, but it was becoming clear now that he hadn't been as prepared for the reality of it as he'd thought he was.

"Just here to help Tripp with the bulls, is all," Scott said, fighting to keep his voice neutral. "I'm not looking for any trouble with anyone."

"Hate to break it to you, pal, but you just being here is trouble."

Scott looked down at his plate, focused on the breathing techniques Brandi had taught him, on not reacting, even as his body began to tremble with growing anger. The last thing he needed was to get into a fight not even one full day into his return to rodeo—the gay rodeo at that. Davey shoved Scott's plate, and it bumped his drink, knocking it on its side to spill onto the last of his lunch. A small trickle slipped over the edge of the table and dripped onto Scott's jeans.

"I'm talking to you, bitch."

Scott's hackles rose, the edges of his vision narrowed, and he dug the knuckles of his fisted hands into his thighs. He forced himself not to make eye contact and let Davey know how hard this was for him to sit back and take.

"Hey." Davey poked at the plate again.

Scott looked up then, and Davey's eyes widened slightly. The little taste of satisfaction, from knowing he'd given Davey pause, felt good going down. *That's right. You don't want to fuck with me.* "Step off," Scott growled, low and menacing.

"Leave it, man," the tank top–wearing cowboy to Davey's right said. "He ain't worth the trouble."

"Yeah." The shirtless cowboy covered in tattoos put a hand on Davey's shoulder. "If you get into a fight with him, you'll get yourself banned."

Davey stared back at Scott for a long moment. "You're right. This excuse for a human being isn't worth my time."

Davey pushed away from the table hard enough to rock the spilled soda that had pooled in Scott's plate over its edges. Cold liquid splashed onto his lap, but he didn't let his stare falter from Davey, didn't stand up and let the old Scott take over—even though he'd definitely gotten closer than he had in a long while. Then Davey smirked, not at all pleasantly, and tapped the brim of his hat before turning away.

Scott eyed them until they were gone, and then his gaze caught on Cory, who was watching him from the line at the concession stand. He stood half-turned, a frown on his face and concern in his eyes, but Scott couldn't tell if it was for him or for the situation he caused just by being there. Regardless, that rush of adrenaline hit his veins again, and his pulse spiked like it had the first time he'd seen Cory. As if that weren't unsettling enough, now he had this unbidden feeling of embarrassment that Cory had seen what just happened. Had witnessed him cowering under the dressing down and not doing anything to stand up for himself. He was in no place or position to fight back. He knew that, but that Cory had seen that moment of weakness sat uncomfortably with him.

He grabbed a napkin and started dabbing at the spilled soda on his jeans with determined focus. Really, it was more an excuse to avoid watching, or thinking about, the cute pickup man.

The table shook again. Scott didn't look up but a low-voiced, half-growled warning rumbled up his throat. "Back. Off."

Response came by way of a soft feminine chuckle. "Easy there, killer."

Scott snapped his eyes up at the amused voice. Across from him sat a very tough-looking woman with steel-gray eyes and a mischievous grin. He made a quick mental note not to ever cross this one.

"Name's Ro. I just wanted to let you know we're not all like Davey and his boys. Most of us in this community believe in rising above our aggressors and confronting hate with love. You're going to have to prove yourself around here for sure, but I think you'll find more of us willing to give you a second chance than not. That you're even here goes a long way in showing me you're serious about earning that chance."

An olive branch. Kindness. Not at all what he'd expected, but there it was.

"Thank you." The words cracked, and he had to swallow back the gratitude that threatened to overwhelm. Animosity, hostility—he knew how to deal with those. But this . . . He didn't know what else to say, how to react. Fortunately, Ro seemed to get that. Her smiled widened, and she stood.

"Just be a good person," she said. "That's the best any of us can do." Then she tipped her hat and left.

Cory gathered his lunch and made his way to Scott's table. He'd watched out of the corner of his eye when Davey had sat down and knew whatever Davey had said couldn't have been good. He'd felt the tension clear across the picnic area.

"Mind if I join you?"

Scott seemed uncomfortable again, and his gaze pinged around their immediate area, like he didn't want to be seen with the femmy little cowboy. Wouldn't be the first time Cory had been avoided or dismissed because he was *too* gay, and he so didn't want Scott to be one of those guys. If Scott was even gay, that was, but Cory had a pretty strong feeling he was.

Scott looked down at his soda-drenched plate. "I'm kind of finished."

"So keep me company while I eat." Cory lowered himself to the bench. "I hate eating alone. It's like being back in high school when no one would sit with me because they didn't want to get teased and bullied by association. I mean, who wants to sit next to the little flamer, right?" Cory noticed the flush of pink that colored Scott's cheeks and snapped his mouth shut. Great, he'd come over here to show the guy a little support—and yes, he wanted to get to know him a little better because Scott was gorgeous and there was a story behind those dark eyes—but he didn't want to make Scott uncomfortable and send him running away, either. "I'm sorry. I tend to babble a bit when I'm nervous or meet new people."

"No." Scott's eyes flipped up to meet his. "It's good."

"Cool." Cory smiled, waved a hand toward Scott as he started on his lunch. "So how long have you known Tripp? You two were friends on the pro tour, right? I met him and Marty last year when he was working a rodeo clinic, and we've gotten to be good friends since, but I'm not sure I've ever heard them mention you. Which you know, seems weird to me, but I guess there was never really a good time to say, 'Hey, I was friends with this guy.' I've never asked Tripp what happened to his leg, either. I just knew it happened when he got—"

God. Could he not control his mouth for more than two seconds?

Scott's gaze was locked on his now, but his expression was somewhat . . . dumbstruck. "I think there was a question in there somewhere?"

Damn, the man's voice was all kinds of gruff sexy growl. Cory smiled and then snatched a french fry, making a point of chewing slowly so he could try to relax a bit. "It's sort of an old defense mechanism. When I babbled, my would-be bullies got so confused, they just walked away," Cory said finally. "I'm sorry. Anyway . . ."

For the next half hour, Cory regaled Scott with stories of how much he loved the cowboy lifestyle and had wanted to be part of it for as long as he could remember. He hoped his endless banter would put the cowboy at ease. "I was five, I think, when I told my mom and dad I was going to marry a cowboy when I grew up. My mom smiled and said that was sweet, but my dad never said anything. After that, my dad tried to get me to do 'manly things,' but I wanted to play with Mom's makeup instead. Wasn't always easy, you know, not being like the other boys, but I had Toby, he's my brother, and then I—" He stopped himself to take a drink of his lemonade while his cheeks heated. "Jeez, I did it again."

"I'm sorry I'm making you nervous, but I am enjoying listening," Scott said. His face remained neutral, but his eyes seemed to lighten a little. "Keep talking. How'd you get into the gay rodeo here?"

"Google-fu!" Cory lifted his arms into a classic body builder, strongman kind of pose to show off his biceps. Such as they were, especially compared to the solid bulk Scott carried . . . that he wanted to touch and lick and . . . What was he thinking? He dropped his arms and picked up a fry, waving it in a circle before chomping down. "I found one close to home, this one actually. Toby drove me to my very first rodeo, and I was a goner from the minute I stepped out of the car. Met Harlan that day too."

"The other pickup man?"

"Yeah. He took me under his wing. Taught me almost everything I know. And then I went to a rodeo clinic last year because I'd heard Marty Fairgrave was there." He dipped his head. "I'm kind of a major fanboy of his and probably drove him and Bridge crazy picking their brains that whole weekend."

"I can see that," Scott said, and then his eyebrows popped up, and he leaned back a touch. "I mean, I can see being a fan of Marty's, not that you drove them crazy."

Cory laughed, deciding he liked Scott a bit more just then. "Don't worry, I'm fully aware how full on I can be sometimes, especially when I'm nervous. Just can't shut up."

Scott shifted in his seat but seemed at a loss for where to go from there.

"So here I am," Cory said, flipping his hands out in a ta-da gesture. "And now that I've completely run this whole convo, I didn't get to learn a single thing about you. Other than you're clearly the patient sort."

"I really don't have a very good story." Scott's gaze shot away quickly. "I was an asshole, and now I'm trying to be less of an asshole."

"Yeah, I'm thinking there's a lot more to tell than that." Cory pushed his finished meal aside and, feeling much more relaxed now, leaned forward and propped his elbows on the table. He rested his chin on his hands. "And I'm looking forward to learning all about you."

Scott dropped his gaze then and fidgeted with the pile of soiled napkins on his plate. "Why are you being nice to me? Pretty sure you've heard the stories about my past, going by some of the reactions I've had so far today."

"And they're just stories until I hear them straight from you."

Scott looked up quickly, a touch of shock in his dark eyes—eyes that were actually a rich, deep brown up close—then shook his head. It seemed as if he might smile, but his lips pursed tighter instead.

"Listen, me and some of the guys are hanging out for beers and campfire burgers after. Why don't you join us?" Cory asked and quickly wondered if he should have done that. Harlan hadn't been too receptive about meeting Scott earlier, and Toby had already made his opinion clear based on nothing more than hearsay. But Scott looked like he could use a few friends, and Cory couldn't help feeling that he needed to reach out to him. He usually wanted to be the little spoon, cocooned in the safety of a bigger man, but with Scott, he wanted to be the one to offer that security, to tell him it would all be okay, that he was there for him. At the same time, he just wanted to climb across the table and taste those pink lips. Tease them until they relaxed and see if he could get Scott to smile, even just a little. He had a feeling Scott's smile would be amazing.

Scott eyed him skeptically. "Are you even old enough to drink legally?"

Cory threw his shoulders back and mocked affront with a hand on his chest. "I am twenty-four years old, and I've had my share of beer."

"Yeah, two beers and you're wearing lampshades and dancing on tabletops," Tripp said as he approached the table. Cory turned and scowled as Tripp sat down beside him. Tripp chuckled and elbowed him playfully.

"Ha. Not true." Cory leaned toward Scott, and in a conspiratorial tone said, "It takes three."

Scott's mouth ticked again in an attempted smile.

"You should stick around," Tripp said. "Get to know a few more of the guys."

Scott glanced back and forth between them. It looked like he might say yes, and then he shook his head. "I don't know. I think folks have had enough of me already today."

"I haven't," Cory blurted, and heat burst into his cheeks.

"Cory!" Toby shouted from the other side of the concession area, saving Cory from his embarrassment. "Come on. Gotta get back at it."

Cory smiled at Scott. "Well." He stood up and collected his lunch leftovers, as well as Scott's plate. "Think about tonight, okay?"

Scott nodded, and Cory bolted, not sparing another glance at Tripp because he knew Tripp would be wearing the same kind of *say what?* expression that Scott had at his *I haven't* slip.

CHAPTER FIVE

Scott followed Tripp from the concession area back to the livestock pens, the ground under his feet feeling unstable—shifting, rising, falling—and he thought any second he'd stumble into a face-plant. The confrontation with Davey, the olive branch from Ro, and then the little whirlwind that Cory turned out to be had been a bit much to deal with back-to-back-to-back. But Cory . . . animated, talking a mile a minute, bright-blue eyes alight . . . and so *gay*. So much more than Marty, and Scott had thought Marty was full on. But what surprised him—no, *amazed* him—was how much he'd actually enjoyed listening to Cory's stories. His voice had a soft, melodic quality to it, set at exactly the right pitch, and somehow relaxed Scott. He didn't even need to understand the words Cory was saying, just so long as Cory continued to speak. Which was as enticing as it was frightening.

And then the moving ground wasn't the problem. Having not noticed that Tripp had stopped, Scott crashed into his back, forcing an *oof* to whoosh up from his lungs and nearly knocking Tripp off-balance. Tripp dug his cane into the ground and twisted around; his free hand landed on Scott's hip. Scott knew logically it was an instinctive move to keep them both on their feet, but the unintended effect was a charge of blood to his groin.

"Whoa," Tripp said, unaware of just how thrown Scott really was. "You all right there?"

"Yeah, sorry." Scott cleared his throat and stepped back, his eyes darting around to make sure no one had seen. "Wasn't looking."

Tripp studied him for a long second, assessing, and then nodded his head once. Scott had the distinct feeling Tripp had come to some sort of conclusion and was about to levy the verdict on him, whether he wanted to hear it or not.

"Just the saddle bronc class and then we're up," Tripp said, and Scott released a breath he hadn't realized he'd been holding. No judgments today. "I usually help them with the horses in the chutes."

"Sounds good," Scott said, grateful to get back to what he was there for in the first place.

He and Tripp set about guiding roughstock through into all six bucking stalls, and then Scott sat on the rails to watch, ready in case he was needed. Tripp stood beside him on a plank; the constant climbing up and down fences when working the chutes was hard on his damaged leg. While each rookie cowboy received last-minute instructions on how to ride a clean eight seconds, Cory and Harlan positioned themselves at opposite points just beyond the chute. Everyone had a job to do to make sure both roughriders and roughstock were safe.

The rails vibrated violently under his butt and feet, as the next horse banged and pushed at being contained in such a tight spot, snorting and stamping in anger. Dust rose in the air, and the scent of livestock, leather, and sweat drifted on the light breeze. A sense of being home crept into Scott's chest, and a longing to ride again lodged itself against his rib cage.

The young cowboy preparing for his ride took a deep breath, settled onto the pissed-off horse, nodded, and the gate swung open. Horse and rider took flight, busting out into a frenzy of tense, high-energy motion. And every time, a little thrill coursed through Scott's veins, as though he were the one on that animal's back. Rodeo had been his life for as long as he could remember, and he hadn't realized how much he'd missed it these past couple of years. He didn't know if he could get back to it after the long break, but just being here now, competing or not, felt right. And this wasn't even an official rodeo—today was a one-day school that preceded the weekend's regular rodeo events.

He watched the greenhorn bounce around on the horse's back. It had taken no time at all for the cowboy to end up behind the horse, his ride already over, and the guy didn't even know it yet. But he would in three . . . two . . . *boom*! The cowboy fell clean of the horse, not getting caught up in the rigging but landing hard on his shoulder at an unnatural angle.

Scott winced.

"Ouch," Tripp said beside him. "I know how that feels."

"You and me both," Scott said.

The cowboy got up, holding his shoulder as he cleared the arena, but Scott's attention was drawn to the pickup team. And one rider in particular. Cory and Harlan galloped along either side of the bronco, still bucking wildly, and Cory leaned down to yank the flank strap free of the horse so they could guide it safely out of the arena. Scott found himself tracking Cory again, as he had ever since lunch.

He frowned. He didn't want to notice Cory, but he couldn't seem not to. The young cowboy's every action seemed effortless and graceful and demanded his regard. Cory sat his horse with ease and confidence, lean muscles flexed with each movement, and every time Cory looked his way, a low heat crept up his neck and pooled into his crotch.

When the saddle bronc class ended, Cory rode over just as Scott jumped down from the fence. "Are you going to do a demo bull ride?" Cory asked.

Scott turned and looked up at him, struck again by how open and blue his eyes were. What was it about this kid throwing him off-balance so quickly and so easily? "No. I haven't ridden in ages. Though I'm sure a few people here would love to see me make a fool of myself."

Cory frowned. "Not true."

Scott shrugged and gazed out at the arena, and spotted a strap of leather in the dirt. "I can't see it happening this weekend."

"Well, I hope you change your mind," Cory said, riding beside him as Scott went to collect the rope. "I would love to see you ride. I bet you'd be amazing to watch."

Scott stopped. A note in that smooth voice brought his eyes back to lock with Cory's. Something passed between them—a connection, a promise . . . a need too long denied.

No. He was so not ready for that, and with someone as obviously out as Cory? Definitely not.

Scott opened his mouth to speak, but the words were knocked off his tongue when something bumped him from behind and sent him stumbling into Cory's horse. Instinctively throwing his hands out in front of him to break his fall, one palm landed on the horse's shoulder, the other on Cory's lower leg. Fire exploded everywhere at the touch—his hand where they met, his arm, his chest, his face, his groin. He straightened quickly, dropping his hands, and turned around to see Davey astride a stocky chestnut, his expression challenging.

"Oh, so sorry," Davey said, his voice heavy with sarcasm. "Didn't see you there."

Scott pinched his lips together and clenched his fists, fighting the powerful urge to lash out with both tongue and hand. *Breathe in, one, two, three. Breathe out, one, two, three.* He recited the chant, which had always worked before, but now he knew he was a hair-trigger from blowing.

"Stop being an asshole, Davey," Cory warned. "He's not bothering anyone."

Davey's eyebrows jumped up. "He's sure as hell bothering me, and I'm not alone. He should not be here."

"Well, he is here," Cory said, "and at Tripp's request, even. So until you know the whole story, maybe you could cut the guy some slack."

"And maybe you could stop being such a nelly."

Cory didn't even flinch at the insult, but Scott did. He'd used the word himself solely for the purpose of hurting others in the past, and that it was now being used against Cory darkened the edges of Scott's vision. An unfamiliar protective instinct rose in his chest. Davey could do or say anything he wanted to him. He knew he deserved whatever the cowboy had to dish out, and then some, but not Cory.

"You got a problem with me, you deal with me and leave him out of it," Scott said, taking a step toward Davey. "Get me?"

By the emotions that flickered across Davey's face, Scott knew he got him. Davey sneered. "Don't be here tomorrow," he bit out then reined his horse hard and galloped out of the arena.

Scott took a long deep breath, trying to get himself back under control, and glanced over his shoulder at Cory. His eyes were wide, but the hint of a smile teased at the corners of his mouth.

"Ignore him," Cory said, flicking his hand dismissively in the direction Davey had exited. "He thinks we all have to behave a certain way and princesses like me need to tone it down so we don't embarrass everyone else."

Like me. Guilt snaked into Scott's veins at having thought something similar earlier. *Fuck.*

Scott turned and caught Tripp watching them from the chute gate, eyes questioning, but he didn't trust himself to speak. Didn't understand where the urge to stand between Cory and Davey had come from. This day had been so up and down, and he didn't know which way he was going anymore. He shook his head at Tripp, and then tapped a finger to the brim of his hat to Cory. Without a word, because he couldn't seem to find any right then, Scott strode from the arena and toward the small area where they'd set up a mechanical bull earlier.

He just needed to get focused on work and then get out of there, back to his bubble where he didn't have to face or deal with anything.

Scott opened the front door and closed it softly behind him. It wasn't overly late, or even close to late, but he'd taken his time coming home, needing to think and settle from the day. Brandi wasn't the kind to bombard him with questions the second he arrived, but he still needed a few minutes before having to rehash the day. The therapist in her would want to know how he was doing, the best friend even more. He pulled off his boots and headed for the kitchen, where he poured a cup of water. He chugged the whole glass before pouring another.

"So, how'd it go?" she asked when he walked into the living room.

Brandi sat on the couch wearing an oversized T-shirt that he knew hung just about midthigh when she stood, but now her legs were tucked under her and a book rested in her lap.

"Shouldn't you be asleep?"

She glanced at the clock on a shelf under the television. "It's not even ten." She patted the couch cushion in front of her, looking up at him expectantly. "Do you feel like telling me about your day?"

"Not really," he said, as he sat down beside her and stretched his legs out, propping his feet on the coffee table and crossing one foot over the other. She didn't push. She never did, and while he appreciated that, the silent acceptance that he would open up when he was ready still felt like pressure. As much as he'd tried to settle before he came home, all the things he'd felt and thought throughout the day were still a confused jumble in his head.

"I met a few people," he said. "Most were cool, but a couple were pretty hostile. Not unexpected—I was actually surprised more weren't. Cory was surprisingly friendly. I helped with the roping and bronco classes before we got to run the bull riding session. It went pretty good, I think. The guys there didn't seem to have a problem with me. Not outwardly, at any rate."

She lifted an eyebrow but didn't say anything, which meant something in what he'd said had caught her attention and she'd cataloged it for a later date. It took him a minute to replay his words to figure out what had garnered that look. *Oh.* He'd mentioned Cory by name, not even registering it, and it had dropped so naturally from his tongue. He frowned as a blue-eyed, smiling Cory immediately flashed in his mind. He cleared his throat and stared at his toes. One day and there was already too much Cory taking up space in his thoughts.

"So it was a good day then," she said and smiled. "I'm glad you went."

He ran a hand through his hair. He needed a trim. "Yeah, I'm not sure it's a good idea for me to go back."

"Why not?"

He didn't want to get into the whole thing with Davey, or Cory, who was a big reason why he didn't want to return. Not because he didn't want to see Cory, but because he *did.* The attraction was too confusing and unsettling to deal with just yet.

"Aside from Tripp and Cory, oh, and Ro—she was nice to me—no one wants me there. That much is clear, and I'd feel the same if I were them."

"It was only the first day, hon." She reached out for his hand, linking her fingers through his. "Give it another chance. I have a feeling this is going to be really good for you, and I have no doubt people will come to love you when you relax and show them the real you."

He smiled but knew it was a weak attempt—he didn't feel it anywhere near his eyes. "No one loves people like me, Bran." And what the fuck did he just say that out loud for?

She got up and wrapped her arms around his neck. "I do," she whispered against his ear. He slipped a hand around her waist and pulled her close.

"You know I love you too." He leaned back and met her eyes—a cool blue that always felt so warm when they were on him. Unless she was pissed right the hell off, then they burned into him like laser-guided missiles.

She kissed his forehead and then shimmied out of his arms. She gathered his glass from the coffee table, and a bowl he knew had been filled with ice cream, and carried them into the kitchen. He heard the dishes *clink* in the sink, the soft steady tick of the clock across the room, and wind rustling through the leaves outside a cracked-open window. Everything around him seemed . . . peaceful, yet everything inside made him feel like he'd been caught in a white squall.

"Go tomorrow," Brandi said as she exited the kitchen, jerking him from his thoughts. And then she disappeared down the hall.

Maybe. But first he needed a quick shower to wash away a day's worth of dust, dirt, and sweat before turning in for the night himself. Hopefully that would help him settle enough to sleep.

Hot water sluiced over his skin, refreshing and relaxing—until he closed his eyes. Every time he did, Cory appeared in his mind's eye. Could he go there? His body certainly seemed to think so, with the way his cock was filling out, thickening, but his mind was a long way from catching up. He turned the water all the way to cold, attempting to crush the unwanted desire, which eventually worked. When he couldn't take it any longer, he stepped out of the shower and wrapped a towel around his shivering body. He still wasn't relaxed, but at least he'd flushed out images he didn't want to see.

He stared in the mirror, just as he had that night when something had snapped inside of him and he'd kissed Tripp. He searched his face, stared into his own eyes, trying to find the outward changes that reflected the ones happening inside. He'd been on the slow boat of self-acceptance up until today. Today it felt like he'd been tossed off the side of a cliff and was scrabbling for purchase. The coming crash was inevitable. He knew that it was only a matter of time before his body took control of his mind. Which meant he surely had to look different now. Shouldn't he? Somehow?

"Stop thinking," he ordered himself.

He'd been worried he wouldn't be able to sleep, but as soon as his head hit the pillow sleep dragged him down. Not even the last image of Cory in his arms, kissing him, could stop the slide into slumber.

Chapter Six

Scott parked his truck beside Tripp's again the next day and killed the engine, but he made no move to get out. Last night he'd decided he wasn't going to come back, but this morning, things had looked a little different. At the forefront, he had promised Tripp he'd work the weekend with him. He may have been an asshole, but he'd always kept his word. More than that, he'd missed being involved in the rodeo scene so much, that a part of him wouldn't be denied returning. No matter in what capacity.

But in the background, he couldn't deny an overwhelming urge to see Cory again, who was the reason he currently sat there psyching himself up. If he were being honest, he'd have to admit the flamboyant pickup man tripped wires he wasn't so sure he wanted tripped. But he'd spent most of his life being dishonest with himself, and it was still too easy to slip back into that thinking. He could ignore things he wasn't ready to deal with for the weekend.

A tap at his window startled him from his thoughts. There stood Cory, all big smiles and dancing eyes, and someone let loose a flock of butterflies in his stomach.

"You coming or going?" Cory asked through the half-open window, his melodic voice drifting over Scott like a welcome summer breeze.

Scott cleared his throat, but his voice still came out in a rough whisper. "Coming."

Cory's smile widened. "Good!" He opened Scott's door and fanned his arm in a welcome gesture. "I'm glad you came back today. I was hoping you would."

Scott fought the little flutter of happiness at that. He adjusted his hat and pulled his keys from the ignition.

"Uh, thank you," he said and gestured for Cory to move out of the way so he could exit the truck. Cory's cheeks pinked as he jumped back. The edges of Scott's mouth twitched upward, but he forced the attempted smile into submission. He did not find that endearing, he did not like Cory meeting him at the truck, and he did not want to hang out with him.

Liar.

"Well, suppose we should get on with the day then," Scott said as he stepped down. He towered over Cory; he knew Cory wasn't very tall, but he hadn't expected such a difference, given he was an average five foot ten. Cory didn't move, didn't seem intimidated by Scott's size, just stared up at him like he was expecting something. For a long, strange moment the world paused. No sound, no movement. Just him and Cory and the overwhelming urge to pull the cowboy into his arms and kiss him until they were each other's everything.

The sound of a horse and rider galloping past the truck snapped the world back into play. What the hell had he been thinking? He turned to close the door, and then Cory silently fell into step beside him as they made their way to the main grounds. The quiet barely lasted a full minute.

"So . . ." Cory lifted a hand in the air. "You should have stuck around last night for the campfire. Ben—he's Harlan's boyfriend—he plays guitar and sings. He's pretty amazing. Oh my God. His voice is like . . . sex. It's like he's got some sort of audio aphrodisiac thing going on and turns those campfire concerts into orgies."

Scott stumbled and shot a look at him. "I, uh, I'm not much interested in orgies." But an image of sexy, sweaty masculine bodies—entwined, writhing, undulating—flashed in his mind. He blinked, hoping to banish the image before it could take root, but he knew it was already too late. His skin flushed and blood drained from his head in a rapid descent. He bit down on the inside of his lip.

"Oh no!" Cory said and then laughed, a lilting sound even more soothing and melodic than his speaking voice. "You were just thinking it, weren't you?"

Now the flush was a fire, and he didn't trust himself to try to speak.

"Don't worry, I won't tell." Cory smiled, bumping his shoulder to Scott's. The contact sent conflicting signals pinging off his internal walls. A rush of excitement and arousal that he wanted to explore rode alongside a lifelong abhorrence that he'd either run from or beat into submission.

"There was definitely none of that going on. I'm just saying Ben has this raw sexy sound that makes you want to grab the guy on your left and get your freak on." Cory glanced up at him, the look coy but knowing, and Scott realized he was walking on Cory's left.

"Anyway," Cory continued, waving a hand in the air, "you really should hear him sing sometime. I know you just got here and all, but it would be awesome if you stuck around tonight and joined us. I guarantee you won't regret it. What do you say?"

What do I say? Scott stared down at him for a minute while his brain tried to decipher the question through a haze of arousal. *Right, stick around for the Pied Piper to give* rodeo after dark *a whole new meaning.*

"I don't know," he said.

"Oh, come on." Cory bumped his shoulder again and pitched his voice an octave lower. "You know you want to."

"I'll think about it." Why he couldn't just say no, he didn't understand, but the way Cory smiled so wide, his eyes dancing and his face so open and sunny made him glad he hadn't said no outright and dimmed that light even for a second.

"Cool," Cory said as they rounded the concession area and stopped. "Okay, well. I'll see you out there." Cory grinned up at him and then turned and went the opposite way once Scott nodded.

He watched Cory walk away. The hitch in his walk was more like a skip.

Shit. What are you getting yourself into?

The sun had crossed its zenith and the main event of the day's official rodeo was about to start: bull riding. All in all, it had been a surprisingly good day, and with a regular rodeo schedule, there'd been more people and activity than there had been at the school the day before. If anyone knew who he was, they didn't seem to care. Even Davey hadn't bothered to threaten him off again, too busy with his own events and showboating for the audience.

Scott had been a little surprised by the size of the crowd—not near as big as on the pro tour, but big enough to charge the air with that same sense of excitement and anticipation. For the most part, rodeo was rodeo and cowboys were cowboys, and a spike of shame carved across his stomach at the way he used to think. Why had he thought these men would be any different? They were still men. They still rode hard, lived for the sport, and embodied everything that was the cowboy lifestyle and mystique. Even the men who outwardly appeared a little soft around the edges were proving to be some of the strongest he'd come across.

His gaze immediately sought out Cory. The top of Cory's head barely reached Scott's chin, but out there in the arena, working pickup and keeping cowboys and cowgirls safe, he may as well have been seven feet tall.

There were definitely differences, though. Most of the spectators were men and shirtless. There were buckle bunnies—but both male and female. The atmosphere felt more relaxed. But the biggest difference had been an event he'd never seen before: the wild drag race. In teams of three, one member would lead a steer, assisted by a second member, and the third member of the team? He was dressed in drag and had to ride the steer across the finish line. It was a camp event, Tripp had told him. Each stop on the gay rodeo tour had at least one. Scott had to admit it was entertaining, and it was clearly a crowd favorite, but hairy cowboys in drag had left him somewhat uncomfortable.

AC/DC blasted through the speakers, then cut off when the chute swung open and the first bull ride of the day charged into bone-breaking action. The rush of the ride, even when he was sitting on the rails watching, hit him just as hard as it had when he'd competed. He remembered the anticipation while waiting for his turn, sliding the bull rope back and forth in his gloved hand while watching how the bull he'd pulled moved in the chute. He'd always been able to tell what kind of ride he was in for by studying the animal as much as he could, and it had paid off more than once.

Fuck, he missed this.

The whistle blew, and the cowboy dismounted without incident. Rainbow-clad clowns drew the angry bull's attention from the rider so he could clear the arena, while Cory and Harlan ran extra interference.

Then Cory roped the bull over its horns, and the two pickup men guided it out of the arena.

Cory looked Scott's way, grinned, and tipped his hat, and a flush of sticky heat crept over his skin.

"Do you miss it?" Tripp broke into his thoughts. He didn't climb up to sit with Scott, just leaned his elbows on the rail, and rested his cane against the fence so he could hook a boot over the lower rung.

"I do."

"Same."

Scott studied Tripp for a second. "I'm really sorry about what happened, Tripp. You had this taken away from you. I just fucked it up for myself."

Tripp didn't look up at him, only shrugged a shoulder. "I'd have had to hang up my spurs by now anyway. This is a young man's sport."

"And a crazy man's," Scott quipped.

"True that." Tripp chuckled and then glanced at him. "You've still got a few good riding years left. You could get back into it."

Now it was Scott's turn to shrug a shoulder. He didn't exactly part with the PBR on good terms, and his previous reputation sure wouldn't do him any favors. Not to mention, he'd either have to hide his real self or be the only openly gay bull rider on the pro tour. The latter was the very last thing he was ready for—if he'd ever be—and the former felt like having to go back to being someone he didn't want to be anymore. "Doubt I'd be welcome back on the pro tour."

"I wouldn't be so quick to count it out," Tripp said. "'Sides, you'd be welcome here."

Now *that* he really doubted. "Maybe." He turned to look down the chutes as the next rider straddled the bull in preparation to ride. "Hot damn. Is that Ro?"

Tripp leaned forward to see past Scott. "Oh yeah. That woman is serious business. I tell you, if I were still riding, I'd be terrified to compete against her."

Scott had to admit he wasn't really all that surprised it was Ro in particular. He'd only met her briefly yesterday and already knew she was tough as nails. What did strike him was that there was a female bull rider at all. She was the first he'd ever seen. He'd heard they were out there, but a far as he knew, none at the level he'd competed at.

The gate opened, and the bull dropped its head and turned as it exited the chute. Ro had drawn a tilt-a-whirl bucker, but she shifted her weight in anticipation and sat that bull like she was one with it. She rode a stellar eight seconds, dismounted to a roar of cheers, and Scott listened closely for the emcee to announce her score—93. The current record holder on the pro bull riding tour was 96.5.

He looked at Tripp and whistled.

"Like I said." Tripp smiled. "Terrified."

CHAPTER SEVEN

Cory and Harlan rode out of the arena with the bull as they hazed it to the livestock pens. It was the last ride of the day and the official close to day one of the weekend's rodeo. Normally Cory would ride with Harlan back to their trailers, where they'd untack and groom their horses, while cowboys wandered by to thank him and Harlan for helping them out of the arena safely. Today, though, Cory had a little detour he wanted to make on the way.

"I'll meet you at the trailers in a bit," Cory said, his gaze on the chutes. Everyone had already cleared out, but Scott was still there, picking up discarded items.

"Cory," Harlan warned, but Cory raised his hand to stop Harlan from saying another word.

"Talking never hurt anyone," he said.

Harlan shook his head but wisely didn't say anything more. He reined his horse toward the campgrounds, and Cory rode over to the chutes.

"How was your first day back at a real rodeo?" Cory asked Scott.

Scott threw an empty soda can into a trash barrel behind the chutes. "Pretty good."

"Different from what you remember?" Cory rested his hands one over the other on the saddle horn.

"Can't say I ever saw cowboys in drag trying to ride a steer on a lead before."

"I bet you'd look cute in a skirt," Cory teased and then mentally kicked himself. His compass might be pointing toward Scott being gay, but he didn't know for sure. He didn't want to offend or make the man uncomfortable. But the corner of Scott's mouth lifted up, not quite a smile, but enough for a dimple to appear in his cheek.

Holy crap. How sexy are dimples? And he has them. Scott just kept getting better by the minute. *You'd better be gay.*

"Believe me," Scott said, a carefree note in his gruff voice. "No one wants to see my skinny white sticks in the light of day."

Was that a hint of humor under all that hot, hard cowboy exterior too? Oh my God, dimples and *humor. Goner.*

"I would," Cory said, but his voice had gone deeper, the words loaded with more innuendo than he'd intended.

Scott looked up at him, their gazes locking, and someone may as well have taken a cattle prod to his chest, the way that stare shot desire through him. He just might fall off his horse—but only if Scott would catch him in those strong arms of his.

"Excuse me." The small voice came from the other side of the chutes, breaking the heated moment, and Cory leaned over in his saddle to see who it was.

"Well, hey there, Tanner," he said. Tanner was Harlan's son, and he often came to the rodeos if he wasn't spending the weekend with his grandparents.

"Hi, Cory." Tanner climbed up on the rails and to Scott he said, "Hi. I'm Tanner."

Scott stepped into the chute and stuck out his hand to shake Tanner's. "Hi, Tanner. I'm Scott."

Tanner nodded. "I know, that's why I came over. You used to ride bulls like Tripp, right?"

"I did." Scott smiled, the first one Cory had seen. It was a little melancholy, but one hundred percent genuine, and a touch of envy poked at Cory's chest that Tanner had pulled the first smile from Scott. But what must that man's full smile, packed with happiness and joy, look like? That was something Cory wanted to see.

"Cool!" Tanner's face lit up. "I want to be a bull rider, but my dad says it's too dangerous and I'm too young."

"How old are you?" Scott asked.

"Nine and three quarters."

Scott chuckled, a deep-chested hearty sound. "Well, your dad's right about that. I didn't start riding the bulls until I was eighteen, but I started on steers when I was fifteen. There are schools for kids younger, but no bulls. They'll start you on the steers or calves."

"So I could start now?" Tanner's eyes widened with excitement, and Cory couldn't help smiling. The kid was about to wrap Scott around his finger.

"Well—" Scott glanced over his shoulder at Cory, eyebrow raised. Smart man. He knew he was getting suckered too. Scott turned back to Tanner. "—that all depends on your dad."

"Oh." Tanner looked down at his boots for a second. "Your dad didn't let you ride until you were fifteen?"

"Didn't really have a dad," Scott said, his voice giving nothing away, but it piqued Cory's curiosity. More mystery to uncover.

"That sucks," Tanner said in that way kids did when they couldn't quite grasp the depth of something. "I have two dads."

That seemed to give Scott pause, his body tense for a second but his voice was light when he spoke. "You are one lucky guy to have two."

Tanner nodded and smiled wide. "They're the best. I should get back though."

"Okay," Scott said. "It was nice meeting you, Tanner."

"You too. Maybe you can you teach me to ride?" Tanner's voice held a hopeful note, and Cory fought back laughter. How many times had Tanner worked that innocent act on him and gotten his way? Kid was smart.

Scott reached out and tapped the brim of Tanner's cowboy hat, knocking it down over his eyes. Tanner giggled and pushed it back up. "When your dad says you're old enough to ride, I'd love to teach you."

"Cool!" Tanner jumped off the fence. "See ya, Cory." Then he turned and ran across the arena and climbed through the rails on the other side.

Scott looked up at Cory. "Did I just get myself in trouble?"

Cory laughed. "I think so."

Scott shook his head, chuckling, and bent down to pick up a bull rope. Cory couldn't put the two together. This man in front of him right now, relaxed, laughing, good with kids, did not fit with the one the rumors had painted. This Scott, though, this Scott he definitely wanted to know better. In every way.

After Tanner had run off, Cory left to put his horse away for the night, and Scott went back to his self-appointed task of cleaning up the chutes. He'd really just wanted any excuse to hang around a little longer. Not for any reason other than he just wasn't ready to let the day's rodeo action go yet. He rolled up the ropes that had been left in the bucking chutes and then paused. At some point during the day, he'd stopped qualifying it as the "gay" rodeo. It was a rodeo. Granted, he'd never seen so much skin at the rodeos he used to compete in, or any cowboys in drag, but everything about rodeo that mattered to him was exactly the same.

He made his way across the empty arena toward the competitors' booth to drop off the bull ropes. Someone would be looking for those eventually. Just as he placed them in a lost-and-found box inside the stand, he heard his name shouted. Not recognizing the voice, he turned to see who was calling for him and promptly froze. A flood of dread tightened his skin, tensed his muscles, and shot ice through his veins.

Striding toward him with intent was none other than Dex Dunn, Billy's younger brother. Billy, who currently sat cooling his heels in prison because Scott had turned him in. He didn't know how Dex had found out where he was, but this was the last place and worst time for a confrontation with him.

Scott stood his ground, schooling his face into a blank mask. He took a quick scan of the immediate area to make sure they wouldn't have a huge audience. Tripp had wandered off to call Marty, Cory was still busy with settling his horses, and other than a few straggling spectators and volunteers he didn't know, competitors had either left or were tending to their animals.

Dex stopped two feet from him, and Scott knew this was not going to go well. Dex's hands were fisted, his mouth pressed into a flat line, nostrils flaring. Everything in his posture read *aggression*.

"Dex," Scott said, his voice flat and devoid of emotion. "What are you doing here?"

"Was going to ask you the same thing, you fucking piece of shit." Dex spit at Scott's feet, just missing his boots.

So, this is how it's going to go. "I'm not looking for any trouble here, Dex."

"Well you got trouble the day you ratted out my brother." Dex's voice was icy and laced with fury, and color rose in his face. "Rolled on your goddamned friend to save your own ass. And for what? Some fucking faggot!"

"Billy's where he is by his own doing," Scott said, trying so hard to not resort to fists like his old self would have by now, but it was tough. His whole body vibrated with a mix of anger and humiliation. "He ended a man's career for no good reason at all."

"Weren't no man." Dex leaned forward, like he was readying to fight, and his voice rose. "And it's no one's fault but yours that my brother's rotting in jail, where you should be."

Scott caught movement out of the corner of his eye but didn't dare shift his gaze from Dex for even the briefest of seconds. Everything in him felt strung too tight, too close to snapping loose, but he doubled down to keep control.

"Tripp Colby, Dex," Scott said. He was losing the grip on his anger, and it leached into his voice. "Remember him? He was always good to you. Was a friend of Billy's and Kevin's. A friend of *mine*, and he did not deserve what happened to him. No one does."

Fuck. No one ever deserved what Tripp had suffered, and Scott himself had perpetuated the hate that Billy and Kevin had manifested into physical violence. It *was* his fault. Not that the two were in jail, but that what had happened had even reached that point.

"Billy doesn't deserve to be in jail because of some cocksucker like you!" Dex shouted.

Panic blasted through Scott. Dex knew . . . but no, he couldn't. The only ones who knew for sure were Brandi and Tripp. It was just speculation on anyone else's part. He swallowed back that brief freak-out, but it only increased his ire, pushing him to the very edge.

"You need to go home, Dex. Now." Because if Dex didn't back off in two seconds or less, things were going to get real ugly, real fast, and no one needed to see that. "And you need to accept that Billy was wrong and move on."

The color of Dex's complexion deepened to a worrisome blood red, the only outward sign that he was done talking. Scott braced himself to counter the punch he knew was coming just as Dex hauled back to let it loose. But it never came. Movement blurred around him, and before Dex could let his punch fly, Ben was there. He twisted Dex's arm behind his back, unflinching while Dex struggled to break free. "The man told you to go home," Ben bit out. "I suggest you get a move on if you want to leave on your own two feet."

"You're all sick!" Dex shouted, eyes darting around wildly before settling on Scott. "You better watch your back, Gillard."

"We'll all be watching his back," Tripp said. Scott had been aware people were standing on either side of him, close, but hadn't dared look away from Dex to see who they were. With Dex restrained, he took a quick scan. On his left stood Tripp, face a blank mask, but the muscle in his jaw ticked. On his right stood Ro, a cowboy he hadn't seen before, and another man who'd taken part in the bull-riding session at the rodeo school the day before. People he didn't know, people he'd just met, and one person who had every reason to hate him, all by his side in a show of solidarity and support. They stood there, in the line of fire, with *him*. It didn't seem real.

"Let me go," Dex railed and jerked against Ben's hold. Ben released him, and the momentum from trying to fight sent Dex stumbling sideways. He pointed at Scott. "You're going to pay." Then to the rest of the crowd he shouted, "You're all going to rot in hell!" He turned and stormed off toward the parking area.

"Nice guy," Ro said when he was gone, her voice dripping with sarcasm.

Scott just stood there. Dumbfounded. He didn't know what to say or what to do next. Even knowing who he was, his past reputation, these people—*good* people—had rallied behind him without a second's hesitation. He glanced around at the small crowd that had gathered behind him and locked on Cory standing front and center.

Embarrassment crowded into his humble pie party. He hated that Dex had shown up and made a scene, hated that he was in the middle of that scene, but most of all, he hated that Cory had seen it play out.

Cory hadn't seen the whole confrontation between Scott and the other cowboy, but he'd heard enough to get a little more insight into who Scott used to be and what he had to face to be who he was now. His respect for the man rose a notch.

He stepped forward and put a hand on Scott's shoulder. The muscles there trembled and tensed under his palm, but Scott didn't move. "Tripp's right. We've all got your back."

"I don't," Davey said, leveling a sneer at Scott before turning and walking away.

Cory shook his head. "He does too. He just doesn't know it yet."

Now that the drama was over, the crowd dispersed. A few of the guys came by to let Scott know they were on his side, as well, and every time one of them left, Scott looked a little more confused and amazed. And why that made Cory feel like crying just then, he didn't know. Scott might be a big man, especially standing next to him, but right then, he looked vulnerable, as if he needed someone to wrap his arms around him, hold him, and tell him everything would be okay. And Cory wanted to be that man.

"Do you want to sit down?" Cory asked. "Maybe stick around for a while? Company might be better than being alone. At least for me it is. Being around others helps keep me out of my head when I'm too wound up."

Scott gave him a funny look, as though he'd just realized Cory was standing there and wasn't too sure he liked it. Cory smiled up at him, hoping to maybe draw one in return, but all he got was pursed lips and a deep sigh.

Scott took off his hat, and ran a hand through his hair. Dark hair just long enough to grip. "I need to go."

"Um… okay." Cory fought to keep from letting his disappointment show. He knew he could make Scott smile if the man would just give him half a chance. Everyone needed a smile, right? Cory pulled his phone out of his pocket and offered it to Scott, who looked at him like he'd just sprouted a third head.

"In case you change your mind about tonight, or you know . . ." Cory shrugged, and a warm flush crept over his skin. "If you just want to talk. Or anything."

Cory held his phone out until Scott took it hesitantly. "Add your number and give me your phone so I can do the same."

Scott stared at the phone for a minute before entering his digits. He handed it back and retrieved his own phone. Cory tapped in his number with shaky fingers and a prayer that Scott would really use it.

"Won't be changing my mind, but there you are," Scott said. He tipped his hat when Cory gave back his phone. "Take care, Cory."

With that, he turned and walked away, and Cory fought every instinct in his body not to chase after the man. He'd find a way to make him smile though. *Count on it, Scott Gillard.*

Chapter Eight

"I'm proud of you," Brandi said, tucking her arm into the crook of his elbow as they walked down the street toward the bar. According to her, he'd had a breakthrough yesterday, after Dex had confronted him. He didn't think so, but he'd definitely felt more welcome when he'd arrived at the rodeo grounds this morning.

Scott frowned and furrowed his eyebrows. "What the hell for?"

"For reaching out to me when you needed help, for putting in the work to overcome your issues and accept yourself, for making a genuine effort to be a better person. And for stepping out of your comfort zone and going to the rodeo this weekend—and going back after things weren't so welcoming." She smiled up at him. "I was right, wasn't I?"

He looked down into her knowing eyes and shook his head. "You give me too much credit; I'm not there yet. But yes, you were right. It was a good thing that I listened to you and took Tripp up on the offer." So much so that he'd agreed to help Tripp again, starting next weekend with an exhibition rodeo and cowboy cook-off Tripp had organized for competitors from the gay and pro tours. A break in scheduled rodeos on both circuits made it the perfect weekend.

It wouldn't be the first time gay cowboys competed against straight ones, but it would be the first time they competed openly. Tripp believed it would be good way to promote acceptance and show firsthand that nothing other than athleticism and skill mattered. His goal was for gay cowboys to compete openly everywhere, and if his career hadn't been cut short, he'd have been the first.

He and Brandi came to a stop outside the bar, and Scott gazed up at the awning. *Chaps Saloon*, the glowing red neon sign proclaimed. Looked like any other bar from the outside—except for the bare-assed chaps-wearing cowboy poster in a window box by the door.

"And I'm proud of you for taking this step tonight," Brandi said softly.

"What's a nice girl like you doing with a dog like that?" someone called from behind.

They turned as Tripp and Marty approached from across the street, both smiling, and Scott had to admit, looking mighty fine in their Western best. Tripp even had a fancy cane for nights out.

"Tripp." Brandi let go of Scott and opened her arms. Tripp stepped into her embrace, wrapped his free arm around her waist and pulled her off her feet, earning a giggle and a playful punch to his shoulder. "Believe it not, he's one of the sweetest dogs I know."

Tripp put her down and pointed at Scott, grinning. "That guy sweet? I'll believe it when I see it."

"Jackass," Scott scoffed, but he agreed. *Sweet* was the last thing he was. He turned to Brandi. "Have you ever officially met Tripp's boyfriend, Marty?"

She shook her head, and after a proper introduction, the four of them made their way into the bar.

Scott drew in a deep breath, shoring himself up to cross the threshold, grateful he had Brandi, Tripp, and Marty with him. He'd never felt the need for wingmen before, but he was out of his element here. All the men he was about to hang out with were gay; not that he hadn't been working with gay men all weekend, but this was a much different environment than the familiar rodeo setting.

His eyes adjusted to the low lighting inside, and the first thing he noticed was the crunch of peanut shells under his boots. Just inside the door was a wooden beer barrel full of peanuts, a large scoop sticking out from the snacks, and small bowls on a shelf above. A sign on the barrel read, *We love nuts.*

Right. He bypassed the nuts.

The place looked like any other country-western bar he'd been to: hardwood floors, wood paneling, 1800s-style signage, warm lights, and a small stage with a dance floor in front of it. Other than Brandi, one of the bartenders, and another woman sitting with a small group, the crowd was all male.

He scanned the crowd and saw Cory waving them over near the back. Looked like there was another wing to the bar for playing pool.

When they reached the table, Cory stood and pulled out the chair beside him. Brandi took the open seat next to that one, and Tripp and Marty sat in chairs on the other side. Cory's smile lit up the room, and Scott swallowed hard, sweat breaking out on the back of his neck.

He cataloged everything about Cory: he wore a deep-purple Western-style shirt with the sleeves rolled to midbiceps and the buttons undone to reveal a smooth pale chest. Lean, sinewy muscles like those of a swimmer or runner caught Scott's eye, and light-brown hair tipped blond at the ends was styled in a spiky mess that somehow looked deliberate . . . and sexy. His jeans were snug, dressy with a fancy silver-buckled belt, and when Scott's gaze dipped below the buckle and lingered for a second, his cock started to thicken. He snapped his eyes up to meet Cory's, and his skin tingled from head to toe. Those brilliant baby blues flashed, and Scott knew he'd been caught.

Cory's smile widened. "Saved you a seat," he said, which earned a glare from Toby that Scott registered and Cory either didn't see or chose to ignore. He hadn't officially met Toby, but he knew the man was Cory's older brother. And from what he could gather, an overprotective one at that.

He managed a gruff, "Thanks," and lowered himself into the chair, hyperaware of how close he was to the little blond tornado.

In addition to Toby, Harlan and Ben had joined in for beers, and Cory introduced Scott to two other men at the table he hadn't seen before, Frank and Jerry. The two men accepted his handshake without hesitation, but neither said much, which suited him just fine. Their indifference was much easier to deal with than the daggers Toby and, to a lesser degree, Harlan were shooting his way.

Everyone greeted Brandi with genuine warmth, however, and Toby certainly seemed interested in striking up a conversation with her.

"I'm glad you could make it tonight," Ben said, his smile genuine. "What are you drinking? First round's on me." Harlan frowned beside him but didn't say anything.

"Thanks," Scott said and glanced down the table. "I'll have whatever's on tap."

"You got it." Ben turned in his seat and flagged down a server.

Cory shifted in his chair so he was facing Scott. "I'm glad you could make it, too."

Scott froze under his stare while a frightening thrill did a quick jig across his chest. Not trusting himself to speak, he nodded.

A round of drinks was ordered and conversation around the table went where every postrodeo conversation Scott had ever been part of went: the day's happenings. Scott took a draught of his beer and chided himself for thinking they'd talk about anything else just because rodeo weekend was over. These guys were all cowboys first and foremost; assuming they'd talk about nothing but . . . *gay* things was a testament to his own lingering internalized homophobia and sheer ignorance.

"That bull is bad news," Harlan was saying. "The way he throws his head back like that, he's going to horn someone in the face."

"Agreed," Cory added. "Did you see how he charged after my horse? I don't know where they got him, but they need to send him back. Cole deserves a medal or something for even managing to pull off eight seconds on that beast."

As with most of the weekend, Cory carried the conversation, but Scott wasn't tired of listening to him talk. The melodic timbre of Cory's voice seemed to seep deeper into him, becoming something his body needed whether or not his mind agreed.

"What about you, Scott?" Ben asked, pulling him into the conversation. "Any plans to get back on the bulls?"

Scott shrugged and went for nonchalant. "Hadn't really thought about it." *Except for just about every waking minute of the last three days.*

"You should," Tripp said, then one side of his mouth lifted in a playful grin, and light glinted in his piercing blue eyes. "Now that I'm retired, you could be the next champion."

Laughter broke out around the table, and Scott's mouth twitched in an attempted smile, but he just shook his head and rolled his eyes.

"If you got back on the pro tour, would you ride out?" Ben asked, and Scott barely managed to yank back an instinctive *I'm not gay* response. That was the old him still lurking in there, because he'd be lying had he said that. *So why did I think it?*

Because Ben had put him on the spot, because even though he was mentally accepting it, he still didn't really want anyone to know, because he was a damn coward.

He glanced at Brandi, and though she couldn't have known what he'd been thinking, she put her hand on his knee and gave a quick squeeze. She may not be able to read his mind, but she knew him well enough, and that small gesture of support was all he needed to be true to himself.

"Shit, I'm sorry," Ben said, his voice contrite. "You being at the rodeo the last few days, and now here, I guess I just sort of forgot you aren't gay."

"No. I . . ." Scott started and then snapped his mouth shut when he saw Frank and Jerry lean in to each other and kiss. It wasn't a get-a-room kiss—it wasn't even more than a short press of lips—but it was enough to stop Scott in his tracks. He'd been aware of the couples over the weekend, but he hadn't really paid much attention to anything beyond his work . . . and Cory. Seeing two men kiss this close and this public . . .

He tore his gaze away quickly and stared down at his beer mug, equal parts embarrassed and excited. He could feel Cory's stare on him and tried not to acknowledge him, but it was as if Cory had put him under some sort of spell, compelling him to regardless.

When he finally did look over, Cory was watching him with a curious smile, teeth tugging on his lower lip. An image of leaning over and doing the same thing as the couple across the table flashed unbidden in his mind. He dropped his eyes to Cory's mouth and, for just a second, wondered what it would be like to kiss him.

Shit, what am I doing?

He didn't want to think things like that. And not with someone like Cory. He'd been nothing but kind and friendly to him, and Scott couldn't deny he was feeling *something*, but Cory was too . . . effeminate. If he were with Cory, then he'd be out by association, and he wasn't ready to be out at all. He still hadn't said the words *I'm gay* out loud—not even to himself in private. But he'd made progress, he realized, when his first response hadn't been to lash out when seeing Frank and Jerry triggered a sense of longing in him, but instead, to hope for the same thing for himself.

"C'mon, baby," Frank said to Jerry. "Let's dance."

Scott watched them stand up, clasp hands, and his stomach rolled while his muscles began to shake. He'd been sitting with his back to the stage, and when he turned around, he saw what he'd expected to see when he'd imagined coming here. While they'd been talking, a growing crowd had migrated toward the dance floor. It wasn't the sweaty flesh orgy he'd read about, but there was definitely some gyrating and sensual movement going on.

He swung back around, putting the dancers who made his cock thicken and body flush behind him, and his shoulder pressed against Cory's. His skin tingled at the contact, and a dizzying flutter filled his chest. He fell back in his chair, breaking the brief connection, but the unsettling sensations lingered. The smell of fresh rain that was Cory's cologne danced in his nostrils, and he had the strangest feeling he'd always associate the two from this point on.

"This is a . . . gay bar," Scott whispered.

Cory smiled, and his eyes sparkled.

Shit. He hadn't meant to say that out loud, and certainly not loud enough for anyone to hear. He was only trying to mentally remind himself where he was.

Scott swallowed, then jerked back when Tripp leaned between them with a crooked grin on his face. "Yes, it is, Dorothy. You're not in Kansas anymore."

"Who wants to dance with a girl?" Brandi chirped, standing up and striking a pose that usually made him laugh, but right now, he was too distracted.

"I will," Ben and Toby said in unison, but Ben stood first. He flashed a smile at Toby, who scowled, and then Ben leaned down to plant a quick kiss on Harlan's cheek.

"Next song's yours, Toby," Brandi said, and Scott threw a dirty look at her that went completely unnoticed. Did she not see the way Toby had been glaring at him all night? Traitor.

"Your first time?" Cory asked after everyone had made their way to the dance floor.

Scott nodded and grabbed his beer to wet his suddenly too-dry throat, but only a trickle teased the end of his tongue. He frowned, looking at the empty glass like he could will another swig into it.

"Want a refill?" Cory asked.

"Trying to get me drunk and—" Scott sucked in a breath. *Where the hell did that come from?* Maybe he shouldn't have another.

Cory smiled. "This round's on me." He stood, placing his hand on Scott's shoulder briefly. Fire broke out under the touch, and then it was gone but for the linger. Cory made his way to the bar, leaving him alone with Harlan and Toby. Great, just what he wanted. He tried not to make eye contact with them but could feel their gazes on him, burning through his resolve not to engage.

Toby took the choice away from him. He leaned forward, his eyes a hard cobalt and his voice even harder when he spoke. "I don't know what your game is here, Gillard, but as far as I'm concerned, tigers don't change their stripes."

Scott's hands twitched with the need to clench into fists. *Breathe, one, two, three* . . . "Maybe I wasn't really a tiger," he said, voice low, tone neutral.

"I really don't care," Toby said, and the tension between them vibrated enough to blur Scott's vision. "Consider this fair warning: stay away from my brother. He deserves better than the likes of you."

Scott couldn't argue with that, and the fight instinct that had been creeping up crashed and burned. "Understood."

Cory returned then and placed a fresh beer in front of him. "You'd better not be being a dick," he said to his brother.

Toby scowled but didn't say anything.

"Sorry if he said something stupid," Cory whispered near Scott's ear as he walked around him to reclaim his seat, and a fresh rush of light-headedness had Scott reaching for his beer mug, as if that could prevent him from falling out of his chair. Then Cory turned to his brother and raised his voice. "He can be annoyingly overprotective."

Scott cleared his throat. "He's just looking out for you. Nothing wrong with that."

"There's a lot wrong with that when he tries to run my life for me."

Toby shook his head and took a swig of his beer.

Cory angled in his seat to face Scott, and those dazzling blue orbs damn near hypnotized him on the spot. "Will you dance with me?"

Scott half coughed, half choked on the drink he'd just taken. "What?"

"Dance? I'll be gentle."

"Uh . . ." Scott glanced at the dance floor and saw nothing but a mash of gyrating male bodies—*oh God*—and then shifted to catch Harlan's and Toby's warning glares. "No." His response had been decisive, and the responding flash of disappointment in Cory's eyes stung. "Sorry. I just . . ." He shrugged. *I'm not ready to find out if I like it.*

Cory smiled, so brilliant Scott could have sworn someone had found a way to harness the sun and store it inside Cory. How such a small body could contain so much power, Scott didn't know, but seeing it directed at him made any discomfort he'd felt or threats he faced worth it. He'd stand before a firing squad without a blindfold just to see that smile again.

Jesus, what the hell are you thinking? Time to step away from the booze.

"I, uh . . . Gonna get some more peanuts." Scott jumped from his chair and beelined for the peanut barrel, except he bypassed it and went right out the front doors to gulp down fresh air. He was *not* ready for this.

The second Scott was out of earshot, Cory rounded on Toby. "What did you say to him?"

Toby lifted his chin. "He's no good for you, bro."

"One, I am an adult. Two, you don't get to decide who is or isn't good for me. Three, you have no idea who he is or what's gone on in his life. Four—"

"And you do know? You just met him two days ago."

"Yes, I do, because *four*, you haven't even taken a minute to sit down and talk to him and find out his side of the story." Cory held his hand up when Toby opened his mouth to argue again. "Don't even. I talked with him every chance I got this weekend. Did you? No. You couldn't even give him the time of day. Not to mention, I saw what went down yesterday when that Dex guy showed up. You weren't there. You don't know. Scott wasn't the one who beat up Tripp. He's the one who turned in the guys who did it. He may have been an asshole before, but he's trying to be a good guy now. So, I think I have a better grasp of whether or not he's good for me than you do, especially since you're basing your opinion on rumors."

"Kid might have a point there, Tobe," Harlan said in a slow drawl.

Toby looked to Harlan in surprise, and his voice raised a notch. "I don't need to know the whole story to know that man's reputation. He's not right for Cory, and you know that too."

"I'm not a kid," Cory threw out at Harlan, who waved him off with a nonchalant flick of his wrist.

"I know the Scott from the rumors is no good," Harlan said to Toby, "but Tripp knew Scott back then, and he knows him now, and he seems quite fine with bringing him here and calling him a friend. You know Tripp as well as I do. That sound like something he'd do if Scott were really as bad as his reputation? People can change if they truly want to."

Ha, take that, Cory thought, gracing a triumphant grin on Toby.

"Doesn't change the fact that I think he's still an asshole," Toby said, lifting his gaze to settle on something over Cory's shoulder. "And he won't ever be good enough for you."

A throat cleared behind Cory, and he glanced over his shoulder. *Shit. Scott.* His stomach bottomed out and a wave of nausea followed. Scott was trying to be better. He *knew* it. Heck, he'd seen it firsthand yesterday. He didn't need the whole story from Scott. Though he'd get that, eventually, if he had his way.

He stood and turned to face Scott. Brandi was with him. They'd both heard, and his heart hung a little heavier in his chest. "I'm so sorry. Please don't listen to him. He's just—"

"Overprotective. I know." Scott's mouth twitched, again giving Cory the impression he was about to smile but couldn't follow through. "Don't worry about it. If you were my little brother, I wouldn't want you around me, either."

"Scott."

Scott shook his head. "It's all good. But we're going to take off. I've been out of the rodeo scene for a long time now, and the weekend's starting to catch up with me. Bran's got an early morning too. So . . ."

Cory racked his brain for something to say, something to keep Scott from leaving so soon, but as long as Toby was there—and

Harlan, to a degree—Scott wouldn't be comfortable. "I'll see you at the rodeo next weekend, right?"

"Yeah," Scott said and scanned the crowd on the dance floor. "Tell Tripp and Marty I said good-night, okay?"

Cory nodded and watched Scott make his way across the bar and then disappear into the night without glancing back. He turned to Toby and flicked a coaster at him. "You're an asshole."

Chapter Nine

Scott pulled his truck up beside the two equine RVs parked facing each other. The site was familiar, and he knew the blue trailer belonged to Marty and the black one to Bridge Sullivan—one of Marty's best friends and the most vocal cowboy when it came to not putting up with Scott's bullshit. A wave of apprehension washed over him. Marty had come around, probably more for Tripp's sake than anything else, but Scott didn't fool himself into thinking they'd ever develop a deep, lasting friendship beyond their mutual connection to Tripp. But Bridge—which meant Kent Murphy would be there too, since the two of them had traveled as a pack with Marty for as long as Scott could remember—wouldn't be so willing to give him a second chance.

Why had he not thought things through better when he'd agreed to help Tripp with the exhibition rodeo and cook-off? He knew the answer: because everyone, mostly, had made him feel welcome, accepted him as he was, and for the first time in a long time, he felt like he didn't have to put up a front. But with cowboys from both circuits, his old and new selves would be crashing at every turn. He really had no idea what to expect now, not from the cowboys he used to rodeo with.

He glanced over at Brandi, who he hadn't realized had been silently watching him while he chased his thoughts, instead of jumping out of the truck the second he killed the engine. She'd come along to volunteer wherever help was needed, and there was always somewhere an extra pair of hands was welcome, but Scott had a feeling she wanted to be there for him, just in case.

She searched his eyes—for what he didn't know—and reached out to give his arm a quick squeeze. Support and understanding in Brandi-speak. He needed it. That small gesture gave him a little boost of confidence.

"It's going to be a good weekend," she said. "You'll see."

He lifted one side of his mouth into a makeshift smile. "I'm glad you came along."

"Me too. I feel like it's been forever since I've been to the rodeo." She leaned across the console to kiss his cheek. "Come on, cowboy. Let's get 'er done," she drawled and got out of the truck.

He took a deep breath and followed her around Marty's trailer. The scene was just like old days, except for the missing poker table—and the extra people. In chairs around a small fire pit, Kent sat with an attractive brunette on his lap. It took a second for Scott to recognize her—Marty's little sister, Lily. Beside them sat Tripp, Toby, and the paramedic he remembered being on-site the last season he'd competed. He couldn't remember the guy's name, though. Bridge was grooming one of his horses, and Cory stood, holding the reins of his horse, talking with Marty.

A flutter in Scott's chest made his head spin, and a smile threatened to break free at the sight of Cory. One week apart and the young cowboy looked even better than the replica in his mind's eye.

He'd struggled all week not to phone Cory, who'd said to call anytime for any reason. He wanted to—more than once—even picked up the phone, only to put it right back down. He didn't really know what to say, had no plausible excuse to call, that he could think of, and would probably end up asking Cory if he wanted to get together for beers. Which wasn't something he'd hesitate over with any other friends, but he'd never been attracted to any of his male buddies before. Well, *before* if he had, he'd have beaten those thoughts down with an iron fist. No, asking Cory to hang out felt too much like asking him on a date.

But after a week without that melodic voice wrapping around him like a comforting blanket, he started to wonder if maybe he *could* date a man, one like Cory. And standing here looking at him now . . .

"Hey, Scott!" Cory's smile seemed to stretch forever and damn near blinded him. Every head turned, and Scott felt like he was standing all alone at center stage, before an audience of thousands. Naked.

Cory handed his horse off to Marty, and next thing Scott knew, lean arms that were stronger than they appeared, wrapped around him. The scent of fresh rain drifted into his nostrils. *Yes*, his brain registered, and then the arms and the rain were gone and he felt strangely bereft.

"Now that you're here, this weekend can get started." Cory beamed up at him, and that voice. *Fuck.* Scott took a step back.

"Might be a bit of an overexaggeration there," Scott said, glancing around the small camping area. Expressions ranged from indifferent, which he appreciated, to a shocked Bridge and Kent, and an outright hostile Toby.

Cory flicked his hand in the air and scoffed. "Please." Then he turned to Brandi. "Hi, Brandi," he said and pulled her into a short embrace. "I'm a hugger," he added with a shrug.

Scott cleared his throat and walked over to Tripp, who'd stood up to greet him with a half hug instead of a handshake. "Glad you could make it," Tripp said.

"Just happy to help."

"I think you know most everyone," Tripp said. "I don't think you've met Kent's girlfriend, Lily—she's also Marty's sister—or Bridge's husband, Eric, before." Tripp motioned to them, and Scott managed a "nice to meet you" to the both of them while his brain derailed and crashed. Bridge's *husband*?

Brandi stepped past him to shake hands with everyone she hadn't met before, and Scott still stood rooted to the spot.

"I'm reserving judgment for now, only because of my friends, but one word, Gillard," Bridge said right beside him, "and I'll put you down." Brain-stalled, Scott hadn't even realized Bridge had approached him.

Scott nodded and watched Bridge walk over to Eric and lean down to kiss him. Scott turned away, and his eyes met Cory's.

Cory came over to his side and quietly said, "Bridge and Kent will be slow coming around, won't they?"

"If ever."

"No, I think they will eventually." Cory dropped his gaze for a second, and when he looked back up his smile was shy. "Once they get to see the Scott I've seen."

Warmth spread in his chest, but at the same time, he needed to step back. How should he deal with liking the way that comment had made him feel, but also being afraid of it?

"So," Cory said. "I'm riding pickup all day today, with Marty and Bridge . . ." He continued talking, but Scott lost track of the words. Didn't matter though, his voice was doing what it did, and with every lift, lilt, and inflection, Scott felt increasingly positive about the weekend, about the people who surrounded him—even the ones less than thrilled to see him—and mostly about himself.

Later that afternoon, the rodeo portion of the weekend came to a successful end, and Scott wandered over to the beer garden for a break before the evening's cook-off officially started. When the day first got underway, most people had stuck to their respective camps. The cowgirls and spectators were more willing to mingle, but those hard-edged roughriders weren't so quick to come around. It hadn't taken long for the competitive spirit to kick in, however, and the cowboys had gone from keeping a careful distance to clapping one another on the back, congratulating their fellow riders on great performances, and just genuinely enjoying themselves. Bonding over their common interest could pave the way for more acceptance, in general, which was what Tripp had hoped for, and now Scott did too.

Tripp had been a smart man by putting this weekend together.

And Scott was surprised to realize he'd been having fun all day, as well. At some point over the course of the afternoon, he'd relaxed and just enjoyed the moment. He didn't stew over whether or not people would figure out he was gay, and the feeling of not really belonging to either camp had dissipated. Cory and Tripp had somehow created a sanctuary in no-man's-land for him.

"So," Brandi said as she and Cory joined him at the picnic table he'd claimed, sitting down on either side of him. "Cory and I were thinking . . ." The two leaned forward and shared a conspiratorial look across him, clearly in cahoots, and then their matching blue eyes ganged up on him.

"I'm afraid to ask," Scott said, taking a swig of his blessedly cold beer. The heat really cranked up a notch in late summer in central California.

"We think you should get back on the bulls," Cory said, and Scott nearly choked midswallow.

"On the pro tour," Brandi added. She and Cory both patted him on the back as he coughed.

Scott raised his eyebrows and leaned back, dislodging both sets of hands. "I'm not sure that's such a good idea. Not to mention, I haven't ridden in two years and I'm getting too old for a comeback."

"Please." Cory huffed and then did a slow perusal of Scott's body that left a tingling sensation on the surface of his skin. Their eyes met, and a shiver skittered down his spine. "You look fit to me," Cory added, his voice a seductive octave lower. "And I'm sure you've got a lot of good years left in you."

"I know how much you miss it," Brandi said on his other side.

"And I saw the look on your face when you watched everyone else ride," Cory said. It was like Ping-Pong, the way the two went back and forth. "I haven't known you long, I know, but even I can see you want to ride again."

"You know, I think that's a great idea," Tripp said, sitting down beside Cory and joining the blue-eyed conspiracy.

"I'm not sure they'd even let me back on the tour," Scott said, but even if the idea of really getting back in the game appealed, there was a new element that gave him pause: The Scott everyone had known then was a homophobic asshole. How would the new—*gay*—Scott be received? The gay tour he could probably join, after the positive way things had ended last weekend. Events like this one he could ride. But the pro tour? He knew how those guys could be—he'd been one of them. Even if he did, he didn't know if could ride *out*. First he'd need to be able to admit aloud that he was even gay.

Tripp raised his eyebrows. "Why not? You didn't do anything wrong. In fact, you did everything right."

Not quite. "You forget how much of an asshole I was."

"You weren't the only one," Tripp said. "Seriously, though, you should give it some thought."

Scott turned to Brandi, whose eyes were alight with encouragement, and then back to Tripp and Cory. The shine in the younger cowboy's eyes, the expression on his face, made Scott want to be the best possible person he could be. Cory's mouth crept into a smile, and that did it. If he could make the man smile . . .

"Okay," he addressed everyone but didn't break eye contact with Cory. "I'll give it some thought."

"Good!" Cory flashed that blinding smile, and once again, Scott wondered again how such a small man could contain an entire sun inside of him, how that light could seep into his own body and warm the dark, cold places.

Toby entered the beer garden and made his way to where they sat. Scott immediately braced for another confrontation, but Toby's expression seemed . . . pleasant.

"Hey, Brandi," he said when he reached them. She looked up, her face softening, and smiled. *Great.* Nothing like his self-appointed archnemesis putting the moves on his best friend.

Toby nodded at Tripp and, completely ignoring Scott, turned to Cory. "Ben needs your help at his chuck wagon."

"Official taste tester." Cory beamed as he stood up. "See you all later," he said, his eyes on Scott. Heat spread over Scott's skin and into his groin, and he licked his lips. Cory followed the motion with his eyes, and when their gazes connected again, Scott felt like he'd been sucker punched in the solar plexus.

Christ.

"Please tell me Ben's making his apple cider ribs," Tripp said.

Toby nodded. "He is."

"See ya later, Scott." Tripp stood, excitement lacing his voice. "Gotta see a man about some ribs."

Scott watched Cory, Tripp, and Toby leave the garden, but his gaze was drawn to Cory's retreating backside. His tight, firm ass—swishing just enough to notice—in snug jeans.

"Cory is an absolute doll, isn't he?" Brandi said quietly. "He's clearly taken with you, and if I'm not mistaken, the interest is mutual."

Scott slanted a quick glance at her and then took in the campgrounds, where chuck wagons were setting up for the cook-off. "We're not having this conversation."

"Why not? I think you two would be good together."

"You know why," Scott said. He took a swig of his beer but came up dry. Frowning, he tossed the empty can toward the recycling bin.

It pinged off the rim before dropping inside. "I'm only just learning to accept myself, and some days are still harder than others. I'm working toward not needing to control my every action to seem straight, thanks to you." He paused and cast a half smile on her. She was the biggest reason he'd come as far as he had. "But I'm not there yet."

"And this means you can't see Cory why?"

"Because he's . . . very obviously gay"*—fuck, I'm an asshole—*"which means people will assume I am too, and I don't know if I'm ready for that kind of attention. I know how cruel people can be." He pointed at himself. "Believe me."

"Oh, honey." Brandi reached out for his hand and squeezed it gently in hers. "People are going to think what they're going to think no matter what. You can't control that, and I'd hate to see you lose out on something special because you're afraid."

"I'm not afraid," Scott retorted without thinking and pulled his hand back. *Yes you are, and you know it. Afraid to stand up and say,* Yeah, I'm gay, so what?

A part of him knew she was right, that he'd miss out on a good thing if he didn't overcome his shit. But a stronger part knew Toby was right. His past was too dark and damaged for someone as bright and vibrant as Cory Ackerson. "It's not that I'm scared," he said, his voice softer. "He deserves better than me. That's all."

"Huh," Brandi said, but she clearly didn't plan on elaborating.

Scott sighed. They could sit here all day, and she wouldn't say another word until he asked . . . "What?"

"You've been a lot of things, but I never took you for an idiot."

"It's the right thing."

"No, it isn't. The right thing is following your heart." She poked him in the chest. "That big beautiful muscle in there knows its shit."

"And they gave you a degree for advice like that?"

Brandi smiled, her expression smug, and he knew why. She was right, and she knew he knew it too. Damn it. He hated when she did that. "You love me."

He couldn't help the smile that pulled at seldom-used muscles. "Surprising, but true."

"Good. Now . . . when are you asking him out?"

CHAPTER TEN

"Dayum. That was amazing, Ben," Cory said, using his finger to mop up the leftover apple cider sauce from his plate. "Best ribs ever. Hands down. You're so going to win this cook-off." His praise echoed around the picnic table.

"Why, thank you," Ben said, standing beside an open-pit oven where he'd been cooking and serving his legendary ribs. He bowed with a flourish and then curtsied, holding out his imaginary dress skirts, earning a hearty round of laughter. Cory sucked the last bit of rib sauce from his finger while he glanced around the table. Three cowboys from the pro tour sat with him, Toby, Brandi, Marty, Tripp, and Scott, but he froze, with his finger in his mouth, when his eyes landed on Scott.

Scott's gaze was locked on Cory's mouth, a completely entranced expression on his face. Nope. No matter how Scott may have presented himself in the past, he was not straight. He may have led everyone to believe he was, but Cory knew without a doubt that the guy looking at him like he wanted to be that finger getting sucked on was most definitely gay.

And interested. *Yes!*

So, of course, he had to make a show of licking his finger completely spotless. What self-respecting guy wouldn't do that to turn on his man? Or, hopefully, his soon-to-be man. He pushed his finger in slow, opened his mouth just enough to roll his tongue around the digit, then closed his lips over it and pulled it out slowly. He circled the tip and then removed his finger and traced his lips with his tongue—and Scott watched every single motion, licking his own lips at the same time. Then Cory smiled and a half second later, Scott's eyes snapped up to meet his. Tanned cheeks pinked, and dark eyes shifted from *I want* to *Uh-oh, caught* and then they hid behind long-lashed lids when Scott looked down at his own spotless plate.

Those had been damn good ribs. He hadn't realized Ben's cooking was as much of an aphrodisiac as his singing, but if he could bottle both, he'd have Scott eating out of his hands in no time. Literally.

Scott cleared his throat and stood. "I'll see you guys in a bit."

Cory tracked him as he dumped his empty plate in the trash, thanked Ben for the dinner, and made his way toward the camping area/parking lot. When he was out of sight, Cory rose and gathered his empty dishes too. He caught a *Go for it* look from Brandi and a *Don't you dare* look from Toby, so of course he followed Brandi's silent advice. She was a clinical therapist, after all. He flashed her a smile, earning a magnified scowl from his brother. If Toby couldn't give Scott a chance, he could just get over it and worry about himself.

Scott had his back to him when Cory found him by his truck, and he took a minute to admire the man's gorgeous ass, thick muscular legs, trim waist, and broad shoulders. What would that man look like naked and wrapped around him, inside of him? His mouth watered. Hopefully he'd get to find out.

Scott turned before Cory made his presence known, and he jumped. "Oh! Hey." He glanced around the area quickly, and a ping of disappointment tapped on Cory's shoulder. "Didn't see you there," Scott said.

"Sorry, I didn't mean to creep up on you," Cory said and stepped closer. Now that he was here, he didn't know what to say. He hadn't thought that far ahead. He'd just wanted to try to get a moment alone with Scott. "I, uh . . . just wanted to see if you were coming back for the bonfire to hear Ben play. And I'm shutting up now because you're looking at me like you're deciding if you should call someone for help or not."

Scott chuckled, but his grin never grew into more. What was it going to take to get a genuine, full-beam smile out of the man? "No, it's good. I was just waiting to see if you were going to go off on a ramble."

"Ha-ha. I know when to say when. Er . . . When to stop saying anything." He grinned up at Scott and got a grin back. *Oh, a grin was a mini smile, wasn't it? Getting closer . . .*

"That's good to know," Scott said, that sexy, gravelly voice sending mouthwatering vibrations into all the right places.

Cory took another step closer, bringing them barely a foot apart. A wave of apprehension washed over Scott's face, but he didn't move, and the hint of anticipation left in its wake encouraged Cory. "I probably shouldn't ask this, but I really have to know for sure. If you don't want to answer, I totally understand, so don't feel like you have to just because I asked, okay?"

Scott nodded.

Cory whispered, even though no one was anywhere near earshot. "Are you . . . gay?"

Scott blinked, and for a second, Cory thought for sure he was going to say no, but then he lowered his head and sighed. When he looked back up, a mix of want and uncertainty flickered in the depths of those deep-brown eyes and clenched at Cory's heart.

Scott nodded. "Y-yes."

"Oh thank you, God," Cory whispered. "Because getting all worked up over straight men is heartbreaking, and I'm starting to get really worked up over you. And well, people certainly would have never thought you were gay before, so . . ."

Scott's Adam's apple jumped, and Cory had the sudden urge to lean forward and lick it. He did lean forward, but he kept his tongue in his mouth. For now.

"I'd never hurt you, Cory."

Dayum. That voice, so deep and gruff, and that vow so genuine . . . Warmth wrapped around his heart. "Good."

He stepped into Scott's space, close enough to smell the BBQ-sauce-tinged breath that gusted across his face as Scott's breathing increased—rapid and shallow. Already-dark eyes deepened, and everything inside Cory piqued in anticipation. This was so happening.

Scott tipped his head down lower, tilted slightly, his lips parted. Cory placed a hand gently on Scott's side, just above his hip, but instead of leaning in closer, Scott jerked back. Just like that, there was too much space between them again. Scott looked away.

"I'm sorry. I . . ." he trailed off, his voice ragged. He removed his hat and ran a hand through his hair. "I, uh . . . gotta go." He turned, closing the truck door and sliding past Cory, as if he were afraid they might touch in the passing. And then he was gone.

Seconds from that magical first kiss, and he managed to go and spook Scott away. Okay, so maybe this wasn't happening right now. But it was going to. He could feel it.

Holyshitholyshitholyshitshitshit.

Scott stumbled. It was almost fully dark now, and he was walking blind in more ways than one. Didn't know where he was headed, he just needed to move. He rounded a row of large trailers and saw people gathered around the now-raging bonfire. Laughter rose into the night air with the glowing embers, while the crackle and pop of fire played as a steady backdrop. He wasn't ready to talk to anyone yet, even see anyone, so he turned in the opposite direction and headed toward the bathroom/shower outbuilding.

He was a coward. He was scared. And he'd almost kissed Cory. *Oh my God. I almost kissed him.* And he'd wanted to. Good God, he'd wanted to. But then that hand on his hip . . . The pressure had been gentle, but the intent was clear, and it ignited a firestorm inside, and that's what scared him. Insta-hard-on. The wanting was too powerful. Kissing Cory would have meant crossing a threshold he hadn't really prepared for yet. Accepting that he was gay was one thing, but until he could say it out loud—actually say *I'm gay* instead of just nodding his head or saying yes when asked directly—it was still somewhat abstract. He could keep it at a manageable distance without lashing out anymore. But the moment that abstract concept became a reality?

He pushed the door to the bathrooms open and strode to the sinks, turning on the cold water and splashing his face with it. He looked up into his warped reflection in the graffiti-scratched surface of a stainless steel mirror while water dripped from his chin.

You need to man up and be who you are. The voice was Brandi's, but the words were his. Realizing he was a coward was a hard pill to swallow.

The door banged, and Scott jumped.

Two cowboys he recognized from the pro tour, Darnell and Roy, entered the small room and headed for the urinals. They hadn't been all that close, but they were regulars on the circuit and they'd shared many a beer over the years.

"Hey, Scott," Darnell said.

"Hey." His heart picked up pace in his chest as he kept an eye on them in the mirror.

"Where've you been, man?" Roy asked over his shoulder. "Last we heard, you got arrested for beating up Tripp, and then next thing we know, Kevin and Billy are in jail for it and you've disappeared."

Nothing in Roy's voice read threatening. He was just a guy taking a piss and exchanging casual banter. Yet Scott fought to keep the shake that wanted to rattle his voice at bay. Had to come off nonchalant with these guys. "Just taking a break, is all."

"And you show up here?" Darnell zipped and flushed, and then came up beside Scott to wash his hands. He slanted a look at Scott, studying him. There was no malice in his eyes, but something flickered in their hazel depths that gave Scott pause. Sweat broke out on the back of his neck. "See you got some new friends too, with those cowboys on the *other* team."

Roy stepped up on Scott's other side and turned on the tap, and Scott hated the feeling that he was being deliberately boxed in by the two. Tension wrapped around him, squeezing, but he couldn't tell if it was real or imagined. He blanked his expression while his fighting instincts sparked.

"Never would'a took you for one of them," Roy said. The tone of his voice hadn't changed, he appeared relaxed—just a guy shooting the shit with an old buddy. Nothing there to worry about.

Fuck, I need to get a grip.

Darnell walked around Scott's other side and pulled a paper towel from the wall dispenser. "Yeah, that's a shocker, but whatever gets your rocks off." He shrugged.

"I'm *not* one of them," Scott snapped, and both men raised their eyebrows. *Fuck! Why in the fuck did I say that?* Other than asking some uncomfortable questions, Roy and Darnell hadn't given him any real reason to lash out. Darnell was maybe being a little sarcastic, but Scott had never been able to read him very well to begin with. Part of him knew that, knew that the guys were just curious about what had happened and what had been going on, and they didn't seem to care one way or the other. Another part of him, the self-hating, self-protecting part he'd focused on for so long had surfaced at the feeling of being cornered. And now how did he retract that and say, *Oh sorry, just kidding. Yeah, I really am as gay as the sky is blue. Surprise!*

Damp heat spread over his face and neck and his skin felt clammy. Still an asshole.

An asshole who can make it right.

"I, uh . . ." He cleared his throat, preparing to say the words he needed to, but his brain and mouth disconnected somewhere in the translation. "I ran into Tripp recently, and he asked me to come help run the exhibition. Figured I owed him that much after what happened."

"Huh," Roy said, reaching for the paper towels. "You sure seemed buddy-buddy with that flashy little blond pickup rider. Guess we just figured you decided to ride for the other team. Still being friends with Tripp an' all too."

Panic pricked at his guts. Exactly what he'd told Brandi he wasn't ready for, people thinking him gay by association before he was ready to be open about it. Would these two go back out there and start telling everyone he was gay now?

"Um, no. Just being nice to the kid to keep the peace with Tripp." *Goddamn it, shut up.* It was like vomiting—it came up fast, sometimes without warning, and spewed all over, making a mess of things before you knew what had happened.

"Well"—Roy tossed the used towel into the trash—"looks like the kid clearly has a crush on you. You should tell him the truth instead of stringing him along."

Darnell nodded and smiled, but Scott didn't like the malicious lift to the man's mouth. "Or you know. You should think about the gay thing. What cowboy doesn't want a cute little boy toy like that?"

Darnell looked over at Roy, and the two started laughing. Roy clapped him on the shoulder. "See you around, man."

When they turned to leave, Scott dropped his chin and closed his eyes. *Why the fuck did you take that? Let them talk shit about Cory? When the fuck are you going to be even half the man guys like Tripp and Marty . . . and Cory are?*

"Well, hey there, Goldie." Roy's voice whooshed through Scott, and he could've sworn his body swayed from the gust.

Oh God, no . . .

"Let me just get the door for you," Darnell quipped, and Scott could almost hear the *wink-wink* in his voice. "Give you two boys a little privacy."

Scott swallowed a deep breath and turned to face Cory. He stood frozen in the doorway, his usually radiant blue eyes now flat and lifeless, the expression on his normally open face equal parts hurt and anger. Two expressions Scott had put there, and now the metaphorical vomit of his earlier words became reality. Bile rose in the back of his throat at the things he'd said. Things he hadn't meant at all but had come out of his mouth, nonetheless. And worse, the things he didn't say when the guys had started teasing.

"Cory, I . . ." His throat closed, choking off his words. He took a step forward, lifted his hand, palm out. "I'm sorry, I didn't mea—"

Cory pursed his lips, shook his head, and then turned and walked out into the night without uttering a single word. Scott knew he'd really hurt Cory, to have reduced the vocal tornado to silence.

Shit. "Cory!" Scott ran out the door after him, but he was gone, and Scott was left alone with his asshole self.

Chapter Eleven

Last night, Cory had gone right back to the trailer he shared with his brother when they traveled to rodeos, instead of to the bonfire party. His mood to celebrate had fled so thoroughly, it had taken his usual need to be around people when he was troubled with it. He hadn't been able to sleep at all, but when Toby had come in, he'd pretended to be asleep. This morning, he'd made sure to get up and out before Toby awoke. The last thing he needed was a *told you so* lecture from him, so he kept busy helping set up the cook-off breakfast and volunteering to do other tasks that got him away from Toby.

Now he sat at a picnic table by himself, having just finished a breakfast that should have tasted better than it did, replaying last night over and over.

Scott had looked genuinely green around the gills when he'd turned to see Cory standing there, but it didn't change the fact he'd said he was basically just humoring Cory to stay on Tripp's good side. That was what hurt the most. Back in high school, a couple of the "cool kids" had befriended him. He'd thought it was because they'd liked him, but the truth was they'd done it just to make a fool of him. "Letting" him hang out with them while they'd made fun behind his back. And the things Scott said last night had hit him much the same.

He was not a laughingstock and *would not* let anyone make him feel that way ever again.

Even Scott.

"You okay there, kiddo?" Brandi's voice jerked him from his thoughts as she sat down at the table beside him. The cook-off had officially ended, and contestants were cleaning up in preparation for the best-dish awards. Most everyone was socializing and doing his or her bit to make light the work, but he'd stayed at his table, in his own little world while people moved about him, unnoticed.

"Fabulous, as always." He smiled, but he knew it didn't reach his eyes—or reflect in his voice. He'd made a point of not sitting at the same table as Scott. He couldn't talk to him yet, but it didn't seem that Scott wanted to talk to him anyway. He'd pretty much kept his distance since the almost kiss the night before, and had not once glanced Cory's way all morning. Not that he wanted him to. Not really. Except maybe just a little . . . which only added to the hurt. But not sitting near Scott meant he hadn't sat with anyone else, either, so they all had to know he wasn't near as fabulous as he tried to put on. *Just busy* didn't work with people who knew him well.

Brandi smiled and slipped an arm over his shoulders. "He's my best friend, and I want to kick him in the ass sometimes, but I'm here for you too, okay?"

He met her gaze and nodded but couldn't say anything. His throat suddenly seemed too tight for air to pass through, and his eyes stung.

He liked her. She was funny and smart and genuinely cared about people. Gorgeous too, with those sparkling blue eyes, heart-shaped face, and long dark hair. If he were straight, he'd probably drop to her feet begging for her attention. Instead, he wanted to throw himself at the feet of a troubled man who would probably end up breaking his heart into a million little shards, never to be whole again. *Oh, stop it. Drama queen.*

"Toby wanted to come over here, but I told him I'd talk to you first . . .?" She raised an eyebrow. She'd only just met Toby and already she had his number.

He shook his head and this time, he did feel the smile reach his eyes. "Not ready for that lecture yet."

She hugged him a little tighter. "I'll work on him for you." She stood and winked. Then her smile flipped, and she pulled at her lower lip. "As for Scott: he's a work in progress."

Wasn't that the truth? "Thank you. For coming to see how I was."

"Anytime."

She turned to leave, but stopped. "Can you do me a little favor?"

"Anything."

"I overlapped offering to help, and now I have to do two things at the same time on opposite sides of the grounds. Would you mind running over to Ben and Harlan's campsite and grabbing the small green cooler? Ben says its outside, right by the door of their trailer."

He stood up. "No problem." Doing something would help him think less. Hopefully.

"Thank you!" She beamed, and a little warning signal beeped in the back of his mind.

A few minutes later, he arrived at Harlan and Ben's campsite, convinced it was some sort of setup on Brandi's part, even though he had no reason to think she'd do that, but no one was there. Part of him was relieved, and tension he hadn't realized he'd been carrying slipped off his shoulders. But heaviness weighed down on another part of him, the part that had hoped it was a setup and he'd find Scott there—a quiet place for them to talk. But he didn't really want to talk to Scott. Not yet.

He sighed, pushing his rambling thoughts away, and picked up the cooler, right where it was supposed to be. He turned and gasped. Shit, it *was* a setup. He stood face-to-face with Scott. Well, face-to-chest because he could not look up into those dark eyes.

"What are you doing here?" Cory asked, his heart pounding.

"Looks like I came to get the same cooler," Scott said, and Cory couldn't tell if there was a hint of humor or apology in his voice. "Cory, listen . . ." Scott sounded more gravelly than usual, but the plea in his tone was sharp as a knife.

Cory wanted to hear Scott out, but at the same time he didn't. He refused to be played the fool. He shook his head and sidestepped left to walk past him, but Scott copied his move and blocked him. *Crap.* Cory stepped to the right, and Scott mirrored him again. Now he looked up and met warm, open eyes that reached out and stalled his intention to toss his darkest glare at the man.

Crap, crap, crap, why did I look into his eyes?

"Please, Cory? Just hear me out, and then you don't have to see me ever again, if that's what you want."

He sighed, and Scott gently extracted the cooler from his hand, placing it on the ground beside them, his eyes on Cory the whole time.

He stared at Scott's chest again, and suddenly feeling exposed, he crossed his arms. Waiting.

"This is really hard for me," Scott whispered, and the sincerity in his deep, rough voice struck a chord that Cory couldn't help but respond to. "I'm trying to get there, to be comfortable in my skin, for my mind to catch up to what . . . to what my body wants."

Cory shifted his gaze to Scott and saw naked desire dancing behind the humility in Scott's eyes. His pulse quickened, and his heart pounded a little faster. He had no idea what it was like not to accept yourself. He'd been out since he was born—that's the way God made him so what was there to fight? Probably couldn't hide it if he tried, anyway.

"I . . ." Scott took his hat off, ran a hand through his hair, and then gripped the brim with both hands instead of putting it back on. His words came in a rush. "I made a mistake last night. Fell back a step. Progress doesn't come without a few hitches along the way, right? That's what Brandi says. But I swear to you, I didn't mean anything I said. Please believe it was all knee-jerk and every word tasted like the lie it was. I'm not ready to announce to the world that I'm . . ."

"Gay?"

Scott swallowed. "Yeah. I've accepted that I am, am trying to stop fighting it so hard, but I'm still having trouble saying it out loud. Just . . . I'm going to fall back sometimes, but I'm hoping . . ."

Scott looked away now, a light blush covered his cheeks, and his Adam's apple bobbed.

"Hoping . . .?" Cory prodded.

"Hoping you'll forgive my slips and be patient enough to stick around because . . ."

"Because your body wants me?" Cory asked and smiled as the flare in Scott's eyes pushed out the last hint of guilt and anguish. This close, in the full light of day, he could see his irises weren't as dark as they'd appeared at a distance. They were a deep walnut-brown with amber flecks around the pupils. And they were beautiful.

"Yes," Scott croaked. That one word was loaded with such need, such want, that Cory fisted his hand in Scott's shirt and tugged gently, urging him closer but letting him decide how far he wanted to be pulled. Then Scott's gaze dropped to his mouth, and Cory knew he had him. He licked his lips and left them slightly parted. Waiting. But he didn't have to wait long. Scott closed the remaining distance between them and tentatively brushed his lips over Cory's. Everything in Cory wanted to draw Scott tighter against him, wanted to wrap his legs around that solid waist, to devour and claim Scott, but he held his reins tight. This first time had to be at Scott's pace, and he prayed to the heavens there would be a next time.

Scott pressed a little closer, angled his head slightly to deepen the kiss. He was still exploring, still testing, but he was becoming bolder with each slide of their mouths. The tips of their tongues met, and Cory snaked his hand around the back of Scott's neck.

Scott moaned, eliciting a whimper from Cory, and dove in, all trepidation flying out the window. He moved closer still, and the hard outline of Scott's straining erection dug into Cory's navel. Hands were in his hair, his hat falling into the dirt. A knee was pushing between his legs, lifting up under his balls, and *oh God*, the blessed pressure sent sparks and tingles raging in every direction.

Any of Scott's previous inhibitions seemed to have fled, and he was giving Cory one of the most amazing, powerful, and consuming kisses he'd ever had the pleasure of receiving. There'd better be more of these.

One of the hands tangled in his hair let go, slid down his back, and came to rest on the rise of his butt cheek. *Lower, lower.* He rocked his hips, hoping Scott would understand the message.

"What the hell?" Toby's voice, hard as ice, cut through the moment of glorious bliss like a razor. Scott released him, jumping back, his chest rising and falling at a frightening rate, and Cory felt like his insides were spilling out onto the ground. If he went with his heart—and other parts that didn't require logical thought—and got involved with Scott, he'd be dating a man in the closet. How the hell would that even work?

"What did I tell you, Core?" Toby strode forward, his posture aggressive. It would be threatening to anyone who didn't know him, but Cory knew his brother would never do anything physically. He barked loud, but he never ever bit. Scott didn't know that, though, and he stepped between them.

Toby didn't seem to notice because he kept on. "I told you to stay away from this guy. He's no good for you."

"And I told you to back off." Cory moved to the side, still a step behind Scott but where he could see his brother better. Scott angled a glance at him and then resumed his guard-dog stance; Cory's heart swelled a little.

"Don't think I didn't notice that you were upset last night and this morning. I know it was because of him." Toby jabbed a finger in Scott's direction. "Already he's hurting you, and here you are kissing him?"

Embarrassment crept in alongside Cory's anger. Why couldn't Toby just let him live his own life already? "You have no idea what's going on, and none of it is your business."

"It is my business. You're my brother, and you're being stupid."

Cory opened his mouth to rip into Toby, but Scott took two long strides forward, pitting him face-to-face with Toby, who was a few inches shorter and no match for the likes of a man Scott's size.

"That's enough." Scott's voice was commanding, cutting, and if it had been leveled on him, he'd have cowered at the man's feet. Toby's eyes widened, but he didn't back down. "Cory is a grown man who can make his own damn decisions and mistakes. If he falls, it's up to him to pick himself back up. That's how life works. We dust off and get back in the saddle." Scott glanced over his shoulder, and Cory fell in love a little bit right then and there. "You're right that I'm probably not the best choice for him, but I swear to you, I have no intention of hurting him. Not if I can help it." He turned back to Toby. "But if you really to want to rail at someone, rail at me. I'm the bad guy here. Not Cory. Not ever Cory. You get me?"

Toby stared at Scott for a long moment, dumbfounded.

"It's time to trust your brother," Scott said, the threat in his voice a little softer around the edges.

Toby jabbed his finger at Scott again. "Swear to God, if you ever hurt him . . ."

Scott nodded. "Understood."

Toby cast one more warning glare at Cory and then stormed off. When he was gone, Cory smiled at Scott. He'd defended him, stepped up, and played his hero, and that gesture right there appeased any worries he might have had about hiding in the closet with this cowboy.

Whether Scott realized it or not, he'd just staked his claim.

CHAPTER TWELVE

"I've been thinking," Scott said, keeping his voice casual as he pushed scrambled eggs around his plate. "It might be time to take my house back." It was the third morning since the exhibition weekend, and he'd thought about it ever since he'd kissed Cory.

Brandi looked up from the newspaper she'd been reading and smiled. "Are you sure? Because you know you can live here as long as you want."

"I think I've already lived here too long." *And my house is an hour and a half closer to Cory's than yours.*

"*Pshaw.*" Brandi flicked her hand in the air. "You can live here forever if you want."

He laughed. "Even after you marry my archnemesis?"

She rolled her eyes. "Don't put the milk before the cow. And as long as he's an ass to you, he won't be getting anywhere with me."

"You're the most incredible friend I've ever had, but what if he's your one and only?" Toby might hate him, but he wouldn't get between them if Brandi fell for him.

"Wouldn't be my one and only if he didn't accept my best friend, now would he?" She sipped her coffee. "Now, tell me. Are you sure you want to do this, and do it for *you*?"

"Yeah." He searched inside himself for a moment. Yes, it would be easier to see Cory more often if he moved back to his own house in Stockton, only half an hour from Modesto where Cory lived with Toby. But that couldn't be his only reason for going returning. Was he really ready to reclaim his life, or rather, start his *new* life? Apprehension lurked in the background. It was another big step for him, but . . . "Yes." He nodded more to himself than to Brandi. "I think it's time. Well, it will be when it's time to move out. I'll have to give my tenants three months' notice."

She studied him for a long moment, then motioned to his plate. "Going to eat that or just play with it?"

He scooped up a mouthful of egg with a flourish and popped it into his mouth. She smirked and then a more thoughtful expression overtook her face. "I think it's a good idea. And three months means you'll have time to mentally prepare. But you know you're always welcome to move back here with me, right?"

He reached across the table and squeezed her hand. "I love you, you know."

"Love you too."

They fell into companionable silence while they finished breakfast, and then out of the blue Brandi said, "So, did you call him yet?"

Scott shook his head and placed the fork on his empty plate. "Not sure what I'd say."

"Start with hello. I'm pretty sure Cory will take care of the rest."

Scott couldn't help the smile that tugged at his lips. "Isn't that the truth."

When Brandi didn't say anything, he looked up to find her watching him with tears in her eyes. "Oh, woman. What did I say?"

She shook her head, stood up, and came around the table to wrap her arms around his neck. She kissed his cheek. "Call him."

Seven hours later, he stood in the parking lot of a steak house, halfway between Cupertino and Modesto, waiting for Cory to arrive.

After Brandi had left for work, he'd sat down on the couch with his phone in his hand, shoring up the balls to press the Send button that would connect him to Cory. The excitement in Cory's voice had been infectious, and Scott couldn't wait to see him again. Even now wouldn't be soon enough. Cory had suggested dinner, Scott agreed, and it wasn't until they'd hung up that he realized they'd just made a date. He'd almost called back to cancel, but the need to see Cory again was stronger than his brief freak-out.

An echo of panic trickled into his chest again, but it wasn't nearly as strong as it had been earlier. They were just a couple of friends getting together for dinner. No big deal. It wasn't like they'd be crawling over the table to maul one another. That thought kicked his mental movie theater into gear. He could see the two of them sitting in a darkened booth in the back corner, gazing into each other's eyes from across the expanse of the table. Cory licked his lips; Scott did the same. Cory placed his napkin carefully beside his plate, and then slowly lowered his hand under the table. He shifted; his eyelids fluttered. Scott got up, moved to Cory's side of the table, and straddled his lap—

Fingers snapped in front of his face. "Earth to Scott," Cory teased.

"Hey," Scott said, shifting on his feet and trying to covertly adjust his jeans. Things had gotten a little snug in there while the movie'd been playing. "Sorry. Zoned out a bit, I guess."

"Yeah," Cory said, then he smiled—a flirty, mischievous kind of smile—and Scott fought a powerful urge to pull Cory into his arms and kiss him until the sun came up. "Care to share where you went, cowboy? Because from the looks of things—" Cory made a point of staring at Scott's crotch, and then bringing his gaze back up slowly, along with one raised eyebrow "—I'm thinking I might like to go there with you. Unless . . . I *was* there with you? In which case you so have to tell every single delicious detail. No! I think it would be best if you showed me, actually. That way I'd be sure not to miss anything in translation."

"You're dangerous," Scott said. Trepidation tugged at him, but the words were tinged with awe.

"Only in a good way." Cory winked and looked like he was about to reach for Scott's hand, but then he shoved it in his front pocket. "C'mon." He tipped his head toward the restaurant. "Let's go have our first real dinner date."

First date. Scott's heart slammed against his rib cage, and his legs and knees felt weak.

He counted backward as he walked beside Cory, keeping himself at a safe *friend* distance as they entered the restaurant and were shown to their table—not a dark booth in the back corner, but a regular table about midfloor by the windows.

As soon as they were seated, Scott's nerves kicked in, but as if he'd known, Cory started talking, as he often did. Before too long, that beautiful musical voice worked its magic, and the world around them faded away.

"And then Jackson called yesterday and invited me to come ride pickup on the California circuit," Cory was saying, his eyes sparkling with excitement. "How amazing is that?"

"That's great, Cory," Scott said, and it really was. "Congratulations."

"It would only be when they're short on riders for now." Cory still beamed. "So, have you been thinking about getting back into competing?"

"I have, actually." He fidgeted with the napkin in his lap. "Among other things."

"Oh, do tell." Cory leaned forward, putting his elbows on the table and resting his chin on his hands. "Leave nothing out. I want every detail."

Scott smiled and shook his head. "I've been thinking, thanks to you and Brandi—and Tripp—that I'll see if I can get back to bull riding. I was thinking I'd just start off with slack events at the last few rodeos this season. There should be enough overflow competitors trying to rack up their points that they'll add bull riding to the slack. That way I won't have to deal with the added pressure of the main rodeo and bigger crowds while I work the rust out of my bones."

Scott paused. Since when did *he* talk that much? Then he noticed the way Cory was watching him as if he'd just told the most amazing story known to man, eyes bright and dancing, and a smile on his lips—lips that Scott knew felt like silk.

"What?"

"You're smiling."

Scott scowled. "I am not."

Cory laughed and clapped his hands together, looking mighty proud of himself over there on the other side of the table.

"Hey, Cory. Scott."

He turned and saw Ben standing beside their table. "Ben!" Cory jumped up and gave him a hug, but Scott only offered his hand for a shake from where he sat.

"What are you two doing out here?" Ben asked. Since neither of them was local, it wasn't like they'd just run into each other by coincidence.

"Just enjoying dinner out and catching up," Cory said, and Scott couldn't decide if he was happy or disappointed that Cory hadn't told Ben they were on a date.

Ben grinned. "Uh-huh." Okay, so maybe Cory didn't have to say anything at all.

Harlan came up beside Ben—with Tanner, the young boy who wanted to be a bull rider that Scott had met a few weeks previous—at his side. Scott hadn't really noticed it before, but now with the two of them standing there, side by side, it was clear Tanner was a mini version of Harlan.

"Hey, Harlan," Cory said and went in for another round of hugs, first Harlan and then Mini Harlan. "*Dayum*, Tanner. I swear you've grown at least three inches in the last three weeks." Cory ruffled the boy's hair, and Tanner beamed up at him.

"Hi, Scott," Harlan said, extending his hand, which surprised Scott, but he raised his own hand and accepted the shake.

"Good to see you," Scott said, and he meant it.

"Same. My boy Tanner, here," Harlan said, placing a hand on Tanner's shoulder. "But Tanner tells me you two already met."

"We did," Scott said and smiled at Tanner, even as something inside of him twisted.

Tanner's smile widened, and his green eyes lit up. "I told Dad I want you and Tripp to teach me to ride. He says I have to wait until I'm fifteen. Will you still teach me?"

Scott flicked his eyes up at Harlan and for a split second, he saw his dad's face. He fought back the old wounds and anger that began bubbling in his veins, fought back the words he really wanted to say but couldn't in front of Tanner. Keeping his voice even he said, "If I'm still kicking, you got it."

"Cool!"

"Our table is ready, so we'll see you guys around," Ben said as he rounded up Harlan and Tanner.

The second they were out of earshot, Scott turned to Cory and leaned across the table. "Tanner is Harlan's son?"

Something in his voice must have tipped Cory off that this wasn't a casual shooting-the-shit question because he frowned and carefully said, "Yes. He was married before—"

"And he left his wife for a man?" Scott bit out, sitting up straight and clenching his hands into fists. Any budding respect he'd had for Harlan just flew out the window. The only difference between his dad and Harlan was that at least Harlan was still in his son's life.

Cory leaned back, eyebrows raised, and concern clear on his face. "What? No. Scott, what's going on?"

"Just . . ." Scott shook his head, trying to tamp down the mix of emotions that charged through him—anger, regret, envy . . . hate. "He should never have married in the first place. It's not fair to the woman, and then to leave a kid behind— "

"Stop." Cory raised a hand and leaned forward, his voice deliberately low and soothing, like he was trying to talk down a spooked horse. "Look, I don't know where this is coming from, but let's just set a few things straight right now so you can relax. First, before Harlan met Ben, he was married to another man. Not a woman. They were together for, I don't know, seven years or so, I think. Harlan and his husband wanted a family, and they decided to go the surrogate route. Tanner is Harlan's biological son. But when Tanner was about . . . four, Jason—Harlan's husband—up and left him. Never really said why, as far as I know."

Scott felt about two inches tall right about then and dropped his gaze to the table. Crumbs from the garlic bread he'd had earlier littered the tablecloth and held his attention. Of course his history would color his perception, and his response had been automatic and visceral. He'd just assumed the story would be the same as his—the son of a gay man using a wife to hide behind.

A hand gently covered his. Pale fingers caressed his darker, olive-toned skin. Scott marveled at the difference, rather than freaking that they were in public and Cory was touching him. At that moment, he couldn't have cared less. The fight had gone out of him.

"I hope someday you'll tell me what just set you off," Cory said quietly.

Scott nodded but couldn't meet his eyes.

"Come on." Cory lifted his hand to flag their server down for the bill, and Scott shivered at the loss of that golden heat on his skin. "Let's get out of here. I know a great place for ice cream."

Scott stood but had to pause for a second to get his bearings because everything felt sideways. Or maybe that was just him.

"I think I'm going to pass on the ice cream," he said when they reached their vehicles in the parking lot.

"Okay." Cory sighed but put on a smile that was almost as sunny as usual. "Next time then."

But neither of them said good-night, neither made a move to leave, and Scott caught himself leaning forward. It seemed perfectly natural for him to kiss Cory, but then he remembered where he was—in a public parking lot and not in the safety of the gay rodeo crowd.

A frown marred Cory's handsome, delicate features, and the light faded from his eyes for a moment. A moment Scott wanted to take back so he could bask in that light again.

Cory glanced around and then grabbed Scott's hand. "Come here."

Scott let himself be led around the back of the restaurant, liking the feel of that soft skin wrapped around his—even the calluses on Cory's hand were soft.

Cory stopped in a mostly secluded spot outside the reach of a security light and turned to stare up at him. Scott didn't hesitate this time. He wrapped his arms around Cory, walking him backward until the wall stopped them. Bodies completely flush, he leaned in and kissed Cory. Kissed him the way he'd wanted to all night—no, the way he'd wanted to for every waking second since the weekend and that first glorious taste.

And there was that addicting scent of fresh rain again, but this time mixed with peppermint from the after-dinner candies that had come with their bill. Cory opened his mouth, and Scott accepted the invitation without hesitation. He twined their tongues, tried to pull him closer, press into him harder, line their bodies up perfectly so he could revel in every single bit of the man who'd managed to get to him in a way no one ever had. Then a hand was on his back, on his ass, fingers digging into his butt cheek, another hand behind his neck, and it was like Cory couldn't seem to touch enough of him. And fuck, that was beyond hot because he felt exactly the same way.

The back door to the restaurant opened with a *bang*, and they both jumped, panting and staring at each other, but they didn't move. One of the cooks opened the dumpster, tossed a bag into it, and then went back inside. As much as Scott wanted to keep going, keep kissing, to follow this thing wherever it led, he didn't want to get caught with his pants down in public. Literally. Because he had a feeling they were mere seconds from that actually happening.

"We should . . ." Scott said, tugging at his jeans to find more room, easing the pressure on his cock.

"Yeah . . ." Cory stuck his hand down the front of his pants, adjusting himself not-so-covertly, and Scott stared, dumbstruck. Cory grinned up at him. "That'll have to do. For now."

"Right."

They walked back to their trucks in silence, Cory's pinky finger brushing his with each step. When they stopped, Cory glanced quickly around the lot and then lifted up on his toes and planted a quick kiss on Scott's lips. "Next time I want my ice cream," he said. With a giggle, he turned and sashayed off to his truck.

"Next time," Scott whispered.

Two weeks and half a dozen "next times" later, Cory still hadn't gotten his ice cream. It didn't look like it was going to happen tonight, either, if the flash rainstorm that had them running for cover was any indication. So far they'd only stolen private corners and secret moments to kiss and grope each other in the parking lot behind one of their trucks at the rodeo or one of the restaurants they met at between rodeos. And it would figure that tonight Scott had parked his truck in the back of the restaurant's lot, out of the reach of an overhead light.

By the time they jumped inside the spacious cab and slammed the doors shut, Scott was laughing. Cory had to pause for a minute and take in the sound he hadn't heard before this minute. It wasn't that he'd never heard Scott laugh before, but this time it was different—deep and rich, right from the belly, and full of infectious abandon.

Scott reached behind the seats for something, his laughter tapering off, and looked him over. "You're soaked."

Cory shook his head but didn't stop smiling. "We should get out of these wet clothes."

Scott sat back in his seat, a towel in his hands. He didn't say anything in response, but the lack of one, and the way Scott paused, told Cory he'd heard. Cory smiled. He'd hit his mark.

Scott took off his hat to wipe away the excess water before passing the towel to Cory, who did the same. Cory threw it over the seat when he was done then leaned over the center console, drawing Scott's attention. Fortunately, Scott's truck was an older model and the console was flush with the seats. Nothing like trying to be all suave while making a move only to have your ribs cracked by the raised console that sat at elbow height.

"Time for dessert," he whispered, hoping his voice sounded as seductive as he tried to make it. He must have succeeded because Scott stared at his lips and leaned forward to meet him in the middle. Cory snaked a hand around the back of Scott's neck, gently urging him closer as he himself inched across the seat and onto the console. One of Scott's hands pushed into his hair, bumping his hat off, and the other settled on his thigh—at a frustratingly safe distance—and their lips met.

Like every kiss they'd shared so far, Scott would stare at him with desire burning in his dark eyes, but Cory was the one who had to make the first move. It was as if Scott was waiting for permission, and once he had it . . . *heaven*. Cory opened his mouth, and Scott responded. Each time he seemed more confident, his kisses bolder, more intense, then there was now . . . Their tongues tangled, and lips slipped erotically over each other, desperate moans drifting into every corner of the cab while Scott kissed him with complete abandon. In this moment, Cory felt like he was the center of the universe.

He inched a little closer, forcing Scott's hand higher up his thigh because good God, did his cock need some serious attention.

"Getting closer, cowboy," he gasped between kisses. "Just a little higher."

Scott pressed his forehead to Cory's, looking up at him from under long dark lashes. Labored breathing, fast and ragged, gusted against his cheek, and the hand on his leg moved. Painfully slow, until his breathing matched Scott's, and he couldn't hear anything beyond this bubble they'd created. "Touch me. Please."

And that big, callused hand cupped him, and his eyelids fluttered while a riot of heat and electricity shot out from his groin.

"Unzip my jeans," he panted. "Please. Hurry."

"Fuck, you're incredible," Scott growled and kissed him on the chin, his mouth, his cheek, all the while working to release his straining erection. Finally he was free, and Scott held him through the cotton of his underwear. It was almost enough to send him off.

Cory pushed Scott's hand out of the way, earning a confused look that disappeared when Cory crawled onto his knees on the seat, shoved his jeans out of the way, and lifted one of Scott's legs.

"I want to make you come," Cory said, opening the zipper of Scott's jeans. "I want to make you shout my name, chant it like a prayer." He tugged the jeans down to reveal an impressive erection. "I want to taste you so bad." Scott's underwear was the next to go—as much as they could go in the cab of a pickup truck, but it was enough.

"Beautiful."

"Cory, I—"

"Yes," he said, and before another word could be uttered, he leaned down and sucked that glorious cock into his mouth. Scott was thick, filled his mouth, and the bittersweet flavor of him exploded his tastes buds into a frenzied orgasm of their own.

"*Cory*," Scott panted. "Holy shit. Oh my God."

Cory put every skill he had into high gear. He wanted this to be breathtaking for Scott, wanted Scott to know how incredible it could be, and most of all, wanted Scott to want him in every way. Again and again and again.

He glanced up to meet Scott's gaze.

"Fuck," Scott said, amazement in his voice. "Pull off. I'm . . ."

Cory shook his head, opened his throat, and took Scott as deep as possible. Scott's head fell back, and his hips jerked forward. Cory eased up, sucking hard as he went, so he could swallow—and swallow he did. Every last drop, until Scott was spent and twitching.

"Jesus, Cory."

Cory swirled his tongue around the head, smiling, and reached for Scott's hand. He wrapped both of their hands around his own cock and stroked himself off, while Scott watched wide eyed, speechless, enthralled. The orgasm that racked his body was the most intense he'd had in a long time.

Spent and sated, Cory let go of himself, let Scott's hand free, but Scott stayed there, holding him, cradling him. "I never thought that could be so fucking hot."

Cory licked his lips and grinned. "Mmm-mmm . . . Better than ice cream."

CHAPTER THIRTEEN

Scott wrapped the braided bull rope around his right hand tightly, making sure his grip was solid, and then Tripp leaned over the rails to help pull the rope tighter, looping the extra length around his hand. Tripp cleared the chute, and the corner of his mouth tipped up into his trademark half grin. "Ride rank," he said.

Scott didn't nod or they'd open the gate before he was ready, but he managed a grin back—almost a smile. "Don't know if I'm strong enough to be considered rank after all this time, but I'll definitely give it one hundred and ten percent."

"Best anyone can do," Tripp said.

He wouldn't admit it to anyone, but he was grateful Tripp was there. It was an off weekend for the gay rodeo, so Tripp was doing his thing on the California circuit. Cory was there too, even though Scott had barely had a chance to talk to him so far today. He wasn't officially working pickup at this rodeo, but he'd offered to help, and Marty and Bridge were more than happy to have him there. The added bonus was having Cory and Tripp there to show support for his inaugural ride back into the sport. He'd have liked Brandi to be there too, but she'd already made plans to spend the weekend with friends before he'd decided to try riding again.

He glanced out into the audience, such as it was. Slack events were just spillovers when there were too many competitors for the regular afternoon timed events, because watching a hundred guys rope steers, one after the other, tended to bore audiences. But every now and then there were too many bull or bronc rides, and they got some slacks. A nice thing about slack: no big crowds for him to fail miserably in front of.

Except for Cory.

Cory sat astride his horse along the rails near the chute panels, and when their eyes met and Cory smiled, a burst of confidence eased

Scott's nerves. Didn't calm them, because he was way too amped up, but helped him channel those nerves into the task at hand.

He didn't want to fail in front of Cory. He frowned. When the hell had he become so concerned with what Cory thought of him? *Maybe when you started kissing him? Or that night in the cab of your truck?*

The bull snorted, crashed a horn into the rails, and Scott forced his focus onto the bull beneath him, who'd hopefully give him a decent ride. He lowered himself onto its back, over his rope, and stared down at "the spot" right in front of his hand. He would be able to tell which direction the bull would go by those massive front shoulders, but he'd still be adjusting his feet and position split second by split second to stay with the beast.

The adrenaline coursing through his veins in anticipation was like water for a man who'd been stranded in the desert for months. God, he'd missed this.

He took a long, deep breath, held it for a three count, and exhaled slowly. Then he flicked his eyes up to meet Tripp, grinned, and, eyes back on the spot, nodded.

Here we go.

The gate swung open, and the massive cantankerous animal launched sideways into the air. And it was pure magic. Never in his life had he felt as big a rush as the next eight seconds. The bull belly rolled, twisting in the air, but Scott stayed with him—grip secure in the rope, free arm steady in the air for extra balance. They landed hard, and his bones jarred, his teeth clattering together, but he was still on board.

And then he wasn't.

He took flight, flung far from the bull—his first dirt bath in two years—but he was on his feet and running for safety before the pain of the landing registered. Halfway there, the buzzer sounded.

He didn't make a full eight, but he didn't care. Nothing in the world matched that feeling of so much power beneath him. The rush of the ride . . . the bigger rush of a successful ride. But really, any ride he could walk away from was successful. The winnings were a bonus.

"Hot damn!" he shouted to no one in particular when he cleared the rails. He made his way back to the chute to collect his bull rope, aware of Cory helping Marty and Bridge haze the bull from the arena.

Tripp was waiting for him with a hand raised in the air for a high five, and Scott gave him one with enough force to rock him on his feet. "You see that shit?"

"You rocked it, man," Tripp said, his smile large and genuine, not even a hint of envy that he wasn't the one out there riding. "You looked like you hadn't missed a day in the saddle."

Scott laughed. "If that were true, I'd have ridden to the whistle."

"Next time," Tripp said.

"Yeah." And there would definitely be a next time. As soon as possible.

Cory rode up and passed Scott his hat over the fence—it had fallen off during the ride—while his heart still pounded like a fucking freight train in his chest.

"You looked incredible out there," Cory said. Everything about him was alive and excited, and Scott had the overwhelming urge to pull him into his arms, hug him tight, swing him around, and claim a victory kiss. But he couldn't because this wasn't the gay rodeo. And he wasn't out.

"Thank you." He smiled back, taking his hat and dusting it off against his thigh before settling it back on his head. "That was fucking amazing. I can't believe I've been away from this for two years."

Marty and Bridge rode up beside Cory, and when they came to a halt, Marty said, "That was a great ride, Scott. Welcome back."

"For the six seconds it was," Scott said, but the smile wouldn't leave his face or voice. "But thank you. There're just no words to describe how that felt."

Marty nodded, like he might have an idea. Beside him, Bridge didn't say anything, just tipped his hat, and Scott took that for an olive branch—or more like a twig, but at least it was a step. Bridge had never been a fan of his, and he couldn't blame the guy in the least. He admired what a staunch friend the cowboy was and knew it would be a long while before Bridge would fully accept him. If ever.

"Best get back at it," Bridge said, reining his horse away. Marty followed suit, but Cory lingered, his eyes on Scott as though he was about to say something. But instead he tapped the brim of his hat and winked before riding back into the action.

Scott tracked him as he rode, marveling again at how agile and strong Cory was and how much he enjoyed watching him work. He turned to find Tripp studying him, his expression thoughtful.

"Cory's a great young man," Tripp said, his tone neutral.

"Yeah." Scott looked down, focusing on coiling his rope and keeping his voice casual. "He is."

Tripp didn't say anything after that and neither did Scott. He didn't know whether to interpret the comment as a warning or an approval, and he wasn't about to ask in case the answer was one he didn't want to hear. Or did. But that was enough conversation on the matter for now, as far as he was concerned.

"I gotta get some water," Scott finally said. "Gotta rinse the dirt out of my mouth." Tripp nodded. He knew when a conversation was over too; that was one of the things Scott had always liked about him.

A few minutes later, Scott twisted the cap off the bottled water and turned to find Darnell and Roy behind him. Apprehension snaked into his postride high. He hadn't seen or spoken to the two since the night of the exhibition rodeo. "Hey, guys."

"Good to see you back out there, Scott," Roy said, as if that night had never happened. "Hard to believe you ever took a day off."

"Thanks, man." Scott took a swig and swooshed the refreshing liquid around in his mouth before turning away and spitting it out. "Felt damn good."

"I see your boy toy is here too," Darnell said, grinning. Just like that, Scott's ire rose. He was too wound up from the ride to control himself, and after that night in the bathrooms, he wasn't going to let anyone bad-mouth Cory.

"Back off, Darnell." Scott was certain the snarl he felt inside was clear in his voice.

Darnell raised his hands in surrender, proving it was, but the grin turned into a smirk that Scott so badly wanted to knock off. "Sorry, man, didn't realize you were so sensitive."

Scott shook his head, clamped his jaw down tight, and started his mental chanting. He would not fight. He would not make a scene.

But he would not let anyone diss Cory again, either.

He took a breath and forced his voice to remain even. "He's a good kid and an excellent pickup rider. That's all that matters. So again, step off."

"Mighty hypocritical coming from the likes of you," Darnell said, a bit more of an edge in his voice now. "Isn't it?"

"Whoa," Roy said, taking a step that put him in position to get between them if a fight broke out, but he was looking at Darnell like he was more of a threat than Scott. "Scott's right. As long as the kid's a good man, and good at his job, what's it matter if he's gay or not?"

Darnell frowned at Roy and then shook his head. "Whatever, man. I was just joking around. Don't mean nothing by it."

"Find something else to joke about then," Scott bit out. *Asshole.*

Darnell glared at him, glanced briefly at Roy, and huffed a short laugh before sticking his hand out. A handshake. Scott studied him for a second, making sure the look in the other man's eyes was sincere, and then accepted the gesture.

Darnell cleared his throat. "That was a good ride, man. Good to see you back out here."

Roy clapped a hand on Scott's shoulder and squeezed briefly before letting go, and then the two walked away.

Fuck people like me. But a little voice, getting stronger with each passing day, piped up in response: *Like the* old *you.*

Scott looked down, everything inside him deflating like a balloon. He didn't know how to reconcile his two selves. Didn't know how to be his true self here, where so much of his old self lingered.

Cory waited until the two cowboys left, the ones he'd overheard Scott talking with at the exhibition rodeo not long ago, before approaching. For a second or two there, the conversation appeared a bit tense, but the parting seemed amiable. Until Scott dropped his head and closed his eyes.

"Hey," Cory said quietly, trying so hard not to reach out and touch Scott. "Are you doing okay?"

Scott looked up at him, expression hard and troubled before it softened. It seemed like he might say something, but the way he held back, the way Scott watched him . . . sent a shiver of unease skittering up Cory's spine. He was going to get "the speech." He could practically hear it already, *It's me, not you.* But Cory knew it was him.

It always was. He was always too femme or too young or too gay. That last one was always a kicker. A gay man telling another he was *too gay*. Which was probably what Scott was going to say because he was the straightest gay guy Cory had ever met.

"I don't know how to put the two together," Scott said. His voice was low, husky, and holding a note of anguish that poked at Cory's heart.

"What two?"

Scott shook his head.

Cory sucked in a deep breath and squared his shoulders. "Do you need space? Time? Because I can give you that, if that's what you need to get comfortable in your skin." And he would, even as he struggled to swallow down the bitter-tasting words. Yes, he wanted to be with Scott so bad it hurt, but he knew Scott still had some issues to work through, and maybe he needed to be on his own to do that. "Look, I can see you're a little uncomfortable with me here today. I know I'm a bit too much sometimes. Believe me, more than a few have told me to tone it down, and I've tried. I really have. But—"

"Stop." Scott's voice brooked no argument, his eyes intense, and Cory snapped his mouth shut. "There is nothing wrong with you."

Cory nodded. Maybe, maybe not, but he wouldn't push Scott any more than he already had.

"It's just . . ." Scott ran a hand over his face and looked away for a moment. His voice barely above a whisper when he said, "I don't want to hurt you."

"I get it," Cory whispered while a little piece inside of him cracked, and when he spoke again, the words felt like sharp glass gouging out his throat. "Maybe now isn't our time."

Chapter Fourteen

"Fuck," Scott mumbled aloud, earning a concerned look from the bartender.

He'd watched Cory walk away mere hours ago, hadn't even made an effort to stop him. He'd needed to talk to Brandi—Brandi with her therapist hat on—but she was away for the weekend, visiting friends in Santa Barbara. Next best thing was to leave the grounds and find a pub. He ended up at a dingy sports bar two blocks from the gay bar he'd been to with Cory and the rest of the guys that first weekend. At least there he could think without the distractions of the rodeo and men comfortable in their skin, like Marty and Tripp, and shock of all shocks, Bridge and that paramedic Eric. He hadn't seen that one coming. But most of all, he'd needed to think without the very real distraction that was Cory—who made him want things he'd fought against his whole life, while somehow making the sun shine a little brighter.

Maybe Cory was right, and now wasn't the time for them, but he didn't like the way that felt. How Cory walking away had already created an empty spot inside of him when he should be grateful for the space and time to become the kind of man Cory deserved. He wouldn't regret anything they'd done together, but how fair was it to Cory to be with someone who couldn't even say *I'm gay* out loud?

No. Cory was right. Now wasn't the time. It wasn't that he didn't want to see Cory, because fuck, like it or not, he sure as hell did; it was that he didn't know how to reconcile the two parts of himself.

"Can I get you another there, buddy?"

Scott stared at the bartender for a second, dragging out of his thoughts and back into the present. He looked down and frowned. He didn't remember drinking it all, but his beer glass was empty. He glanced at his watch, surprised to see how late it had gotten.

"Nah, I'm good," he said, gathering his things as he stood.

He stepped out onto the sidewalk and took in a deep breath of refreshing air. The sun had gone down, and this time of year the nights were getting cool enough for an extra layer of clothing. Or a brisk stroll. He'd parked his truck several blocks away, knowing he'd need the walk after a drink or two. But instead of going anywhere, he pulled his phone out of his pocket and scrolled through his contacts until he came to Cory's name. He stared at it for a long moment, thumb hovering over the Send button.

Yes, no, yes, no. C'mon Gillard. Grab some balls. He chuckled at that last thought. Somehow it had taken on a whole new meaning, which led to thinking about another man's balls—one pair in particular that he actually wouldn't mind grabbing at all.

Okay, you're going to press Se—

A shouted slur drew his attention, followed by a pained sound. He shoved the phone back in his pocket and quickly walked around the corner but didn't see anything. Another shout. Words Scott himself had used at one time but that now made guilt push years of angry bile into the back of his throat. He knew there was a small alley between two buildings just ahead and picked up his pace.

He rounded the alley in time to see two men shove another against the brick wall, face-first.

"Hold his arms," the taller of the two aggressors said. When the second man yanked their victim's arms behind his back and swung him around to face the first, exposed and vulnerable, Scott's heart stopped.

Cory.

Red clouded the edges of his vision.

Those fucking assholes had Cory.

He fisted his hands so tight his nails dug sharply into his palms.

"Let him go!"

All three heads turned at his shout. Surprise on the two assholes' faces—the taller of which turned out to be Dex—but Cory's was a mix of fear and pain, and Scott wanted to hurt those men like he'd never wanted to hurt someone before. He wanted to crush them, see them bleed.

He thought he might have heard his name, but it was too hard to hear over the roaring in his ears, to focus on anything other than getting Cory to safety and seeking vengeance for anyone daring to harm to him.

The two men let Cory go, jumping back as Scott charged down the alley toward them. He pulled Cory behind him, and then his fist connected with the closest jaw. Dex's head rocked from the force of the blow. He stumbled, shock on his face, and fell to the filthy pavement. The other man looked for an escape, but the only way out of the alley was past Scott, and the asshole seemed at least smart enough to realize that wasn't a good idea.

"What the fuck?" Dex said, swiping his face with a shirtsleeve that came away bloody. "He's just a fucking faggot."

Every muscle in Scott's body twitched with the need to fight. "No. He's a human being, you dumb fuck!" He stepped forward, raising his fists, as Dex pushed himself back up to his feet, but a gentle hand on his biceps stilled him. He glanced over his shoulder and was met with wide blue eyes shining with unshed tears.

"No more. Please." Cory's voice was ragged, strained, but the plea was as loud as a siren bell. The blind rage that had him wanting to do more than just hurt ebbed. He would not cause Cory any more anguish, even if it meant letting these two assholes walk away.

"One of the best I've ever known," Scott said to him quietly.

Then he turned back to the men, his jaw clenching as he tried to keep from bashing their faces in. "And you two," he bit out, "are pieces of shit."

"I know who you are," the man Scott didn't recognize said. "What the fuck happened to you? You've changed."

"Yes, I have. Thank God." Scott leaned forward, letting his rage rise up again, focusing it full force on the two cowboys. "I see either of you near him again, or doing anything like this to anyone else, and you'll see the Scott you remember up close and personal. You'll wish you never crossed his path. Get me?"

The one guy nodded, but Dex glared back. "What are you going to do? Rat me out like you did my brother? For a fa—"

Scott stepped right into Dex's space, forcing him backward. His muscles twitched and his vision flashed red. "Say it and I will put you down right now. There won't be anything left of you to arrest," Scott said, his voice low, controlled, menacing. "Now get the fuck out of here before I change my mind."

The nameless asshole turned tail and ran, and then Dex joined him after leveling one more glare at Scott. The two ran like the cowards they were, with their fucking tails between their legs.

When they disappeared around the building, Scott turned to Cory. "Are you okay?"

Cory nodded, crossed his arms, and lifted his chin. He was shaking, his shirt was torn, and there was a long scrape on his cheek from the rough brick of the wall he'd been shoved into. Fortunately, it didn't seem deep. And even as he appeared on the verge of shattering, he held himself together.

"I'm sorry," he said, his chin trembling.

"What the hell do you have to be sorry for?"

"I saw your truck and was looking for you. Those guys jumped me." Cory looked away, as if he couldn't hold Scott's gaze. "I shouldn't even be here, not after I said I'd give you space, but . . . I wanted to see you so bad. Then I worried I wouldn't and—"

"Ah, Cory." Scott couldn't take it anymore, not with Cory standing right there and breaking apart. He closed the short distance between them and wrapped his arms around Cory, pulling him as close as possible, holding him tight, sheltering him while he shook. Scott didn't care that someone could walk by at any second and see them. This growing need to protect, to comfort, to care for Cory was far stronger than his worries about being outed before he was ready. Whatever happened to him didn't matter, but making sure Cory's light never dimmed . . . Somewhere along the way that had become the most important thing. He might not be the best man for Cory, but he sure as hell would try to be.

"I'm just glad I left the bar when I did, and you weren't hurt worse," Scott said.

Cory yanked himself out of Scott's embrace and stood to his full height, such as it was, eyes burning with the anger that welled up inside. "Great. Thanks," he snapped. "Because I'm not man enough to take care of myself, right?"

"What? No, Cory." Scott's eyes were wide and his hands in the air. "That's not what I said."

"Sure it is." The trembling of Cory's body rattled his voice, which only pissed him off more. "You just said if you hadn't happened along, I'd have been beat up worse. Thanks for the vote of confidence."

"There were two of them."

"Yeah, and you took them on, didn't you?"

"I—" Scott's jaw worked, but no words came from his mouth.

Cory threw his arms up. "Exactly."

"I probably have close to a hundred pounds on you."

"My point again." Cory was done. Done with people thinking he was just some little pansy boy. He turned and stormed out of the alley, heading right. Then stopped for a moment, forgetting where he'd parked his truck. *No. The other way, I think.* How could he be so turned around in a familiar area?

He started walking in the other direction, and three strides later, Scott was at his side, silent but matching his pace.

"I'm not like Toby," Scott finally said, and Cory snorted. "And I don't think you can't take care of yourself or aren't strong enough or anything like that."

Cory didn't look at Scott, though he watched him from the corner of his eye. *Jeez, how long is this block*? He didn't remember having walked so far before he got jumped.

"I watch you when you work pickup," Scott said, his voice quiet with the confession. "I marvel at how strong you are, how graceful in the saddle you are, how *alive* you are."

Some of Cory's anger leached out into the cool night air, and he shivered. Why did Scott have to go and say stuff like that? He wouldn't be able to stay angry if Scott kept that up. Why was he even mad at Scott in the first place? He stopped at a corner, and Scott stayed with him, quiet and patient.

Neither direction looked familiar, but now he didn't want to turn around and go back for fear he'd look more like the idiot he was. He mentally flipped a coin and turned left.

"Strength comes in all kinds of forms," Scott continued, his voice that same soft seduction. "I might have bigger muscles, but you are far stronger and braver than I will ever be."

"Please," Cory said, but there wasn't any fire in his voice. He folded his arms over his chest, hoping to retain a little body heat as the temperature felt like it just dropped ten degrees. Maybe he was going into shock from the altercation, now that the adrenaline that had been coursing through his veins began to dissipate. He stopped at the next street. Where the hell was he?

"I didn't mean to make you feel like you couldn't have looked after yourself, but when I saw who those guys were pushing around . . ." Scott trailed off, and Cory saw him dip his head, but he fought back prodding Scott to continue. "I care about you, Cory. You could be four foot nine and eighty pounds, or seven feet tall and three hundred, and I would still charge in like that. I won't let anyone hurt you in any way. Not if I can help it."

Cory stopped and turned to face him. "So, you're saying?"

"Sometimes people do things for us not because we can't do them ourselves, but because they want to make sure we always have a reason to smile, or we have a better life than they did."

Shit. He stopped and dropped his chin to his chest. Scott was right. He'd have done the same thing if the situation were reversed. Now what did he say?

"By the way, where are you going?" Scott asked.

Cory huffed, and a tremor shook his body. "I lost my truck."

Instead of the laughter he'd expected, a finger tucked under his chin, gently, silently, asking him to look up. When he did, Scott placed a soft kiss on his eyebrow, then the other, then his nose, his uninjured cheek, and finally on his lips.

"Come on," Scott said, reaching for Cory's hand and holding it tight. "Let me take you home with me, please?"

"My truck."

"You don't know where it is." Scott smiled, but it was a gentle smile, not mocking. "We'll come back for it tomorrow. Okay?"

The fight completely gone from him now, Cory didn't argue or question, just nodded and quietly said, "Okay."

Chapter Fifteen

After a long hot shower and a change into clean but oversized clothing, Cory followed his nose into the kitchen. Scott stood at the stove with his back to him, stirring whatever was in the pot that gave off such a homey scent. He pulled up a chair at the granite-topped island, and Scott looked over his shoulder. He smiled, warm and welcoming.

"Hey," Scott said, returning to the stove and flicking off the element. "Feel better?"

"Yes, thank you." He did feel a little better, even though tremors still lingered under his skin and his cheek had begun to ache. He'd have a nice little bruise there in the morning. But being here with Scott, wrapped in soft cotton that smelled of cowboy and mint, was worth what had happened. Mostly. In some weird way that made sense to him.

"Chicken noodle soup," Scott said, pouring the steaming hot liquid into a bowl. He placed it on the counter in front of him. "Cures all ails, my dad used to say when I was a ki—" Scott turned to grab a spoon and a box of crackers, but Cory didn't miss the frown on his face.

"Eat," Scott said, sliding the spoon and crackers next to the bowl.

Cory wasn't hungry. The last thing on his mind was food, but the flavorful aroma of the noodle soup teased his senses, and his stomach grumbled. Scott grinned and sat down in a chair across the island from him. "You're not eating, too?"

Scott shook his head. "I had some toast when you were in the shower."

"Hardly a meal fit for a cowboy," Cory teased, but Scott only smiled in response. That smile—it was small, a touch melancholy, but it was as transforming as Cory knew it would be. It smoothed all the hard edges and made Scott that much more attractive. Now he just needed the smile to reach his eyes. Right now Cory couldn't quite read the look in those darkly warm orbs. Concern? Regret, maybe? But there was something else swimming around in their depths. Not so much desire, exactly, but . . . affection. And just like that, Cory felt like he could fly.

Scott shifted in his seat and looked down at the counter, breaking their long stare. "So, uh . . . there's clean sheets on the bed in the spare room. Brandi makes sure it's always ready for guests. Sleep as long as you want. I'll be just down the hall if you need anything."

"What if I need you?" Cory whispered and pinched his tongue between his teeth. He hadn't meant for the thought to actually spill out into the open. But Scott's cheeks pinked, and Cory leaned forward, sliding his hand across the surface of the counter until his fingertips met the back of Scott's hand.

Scott stared at the place where their skin connected for a second, then he stood and went about cleaning up his cooking mess. Not that soup from a can made much of a mess. "Might be a good idea to just get a good rest tonight." His gravelly voice carried a hint of trepidation in it.

Too much, too soon.

"Yeah. You're right." He looked down at his bowl. Now empty. "Sorry."

He stood and then Scott was right in front of him, one hand on his hip, the other gently cupping the side of his face that didn't get scraped up. "I'm working my way there, okay?"

Cory nodded, oddly humbled by the naked honesty in those dark eyes. He stepped closer, into Scott's space, and Scott wrapped his arms around him. Yes, that was where he needed to be. But it was over too soon. Scott leaned back and kissed him tenderly on the mouth.

"Come on," he said, taking Cory's hand in his and leading him to the guest room. "Let's call this day done."

But three hours later, the day still wasn't done. Every time Cory closed his eyes, he saw those two guys and the fear rose, as if it were happening all over again right at that moment. He rolled to his side and stared at the door. Scott was a short skip down the hall. Would he be asleep or still awake like him, tossing and turning for reasons of his own?

Somewhere in the distance a car backfired, and Cory's heart launched into his throat. He could not do this. He would never get a single minute of sleep alone in this strange room when the man he wanted, who'd come to his rescue like some sort of knight in shining armor, who made him feel safe in a way no one had before, lay just a room away.

Cory slipped out of bed and quietly tiptoed down the hall. He pushed the door open and whispered, "Scott?" but the only sound that greeted him was the soft snuffles of someone deep in sleep. A sliver of moonlight shone through the open window blinds and painted a line across a bare torso.

Cory gently closed the door, crossed the room. He crawled under the covers, putting his naked back to Scott's bare chest. Scott mumbled, hot moist breath puffed over Cory's shoulder, and then a strong arm snaked around his middle, tugging him closer. Cory curled himself deeper into the cocoon of Scott's muscular body and sighed. Finally he felt safe, finally he was protected, and finally, only minutes later, sweet slumber pulled him under.

The first thing Scott became aware of when consciousness crept in was the sun warming his eyelids and hair tickling his nose. The second thing was the press of a lean body tucked into his, and a firm backside cradling his morning wood. He hummed and rolled his hips forward lazily, and then froze at the answering *hmm*. He'd gone to bed alone and hadn't drank anywhere near enough to not remember bringing someone home. His eyes snapped open.

He'd brought Cory home.

But Cory had gone to sleep in the guest room. Or so he'd thought.

Scott tried to move back slowly, trying not to disturb Cory while putting more space between them, but a foot hooked around his ankle and the arm he'd draped over his middle was captured and pulled up under Cory's chin.

"Cory . . ."

"Shh." Cory's voice was sleep heavy but still had that same melodically soothing tone to it. "Let's just lie like this for a while. Please?"

It was the *please* that made Scott close his eyes and press a kiss to Cory's shoulder.

"I couldn't sleep," Cory said quietly. "Every time I closed my eyes, I saw them. Then I'd look around the room to make sure I wasn't still there, but everything was different, and I felt all disoriented for a few seconds. And . . ." Cory glanced over his shoulder and met Scott's gaze. "And I just really want to be with you."

"So do I," Scott whispered. The words left him feeling raw, vulnerable—scared—but it was the truth. Just having Cory there, tucked next to him, felt right. Like coming home.

"In every way," Cory added. His voice was lower, the words heavier, his stare intense and he rocked his butt against Scott's groin. Scott's heart leapt into his throat and lodged there. Was that what Cory wanted? Now?

It wasn't that he didn't want Cory like that too, because right now, with the way his blood pulsed southward, filling his cock, he definitely did. It wasn't as if he'd never had anal sex before either. But that was the rub. They'd kissed, they'd groped, and Cory had given him head like no one ever, but he hadn't even seen Cory's cock, let alone sucked it—didn't even know if he could—and now he was thinking about doing a whole lot more with him?

"Close your eyes," Cory said.

"What?"

"Close your eyes," Cory repeated, turning in Scott's arms to face him. Those big beautiful eyes looked up at him with more adoration than he was worthy of. "I can hear you thinking so loud I'm worried your brains are going to start leaking out your ears. So, I'm going to help you stop thinking and start feeling."

"But . . . I . . ."

"You're afraid of what you might feel?" Cory asked, and Scott nodded. What if he loved it? What if he hated it? What if he hurt Cory?

"Trust me, okay?" Cory traced the curve of his jaw with two fingertips.

If there was anyone he knew he could trust implicitly, it was Cory. And he did want this. His body sure as hell did, and maybe it was past time for his brain to start catching up. Cory could help him cross that last threshold. Scott had to clear his throat a couple of times before he could speak. "Okay."

He closed his eyes and exhaled a long, shaky breath . . . and waited.

The fingers that had been tracing his jaw became a hand cupping his cheek. Hot breath drifted over his mouth, the only warning before soft lips caressed his. The kiss was slow, tender . . . loving. He angled his head and opened his mouth, inviting Cory in deeper. Cory didn't hesitate, his tongue sliding inside to tangle with his own, and Scott couldn't remember simply kissing someone quite so much before. He'd always enjoyed kissing, but kissing Cory was so much . . . more. Was it because he was a man or because he was Cory? Both, if he were honest with himself.

Cory shifted his body closer to Scott's from shoulder to toe. A foot slid between his legs while the hand that had been caressing his cheek slowly moved down his neck, over his shoulder, over his pec to lightly pinch a nipple. A zing of electricity shot in every direction as he moaned into Cory's mouth.

"That's it," Cory whispered against his lips. "Just feel."

And then his hand was being guided to Cory's hip. "Follow me," Cory said.

Scott didn't know what he meant for a second, until Cory's hand was back on him in the same place, moving in small circles around the hipbone, the glute, the upper thigh, and Scott got it. He moved his own hand over the sharp angle of Cory's hipbone. While Scott was naked—he wasn't one for sleeping with clothing restricting him in any way—Cory was wearing briefs. And Scott suddenly needed to get them out of his way. He slipped his hand under the band, and up along the side of Cory's butt cheek, the skin there so soft and smooth.

Cory stopped. "Lead me," he whispered.

Scott almost asked how, but Cory's words echoed in his mind: *Just feel.*

And so he did. He traced his hand over Cory's rib cage, and Cory's hand did the same, ghosting Scott's rib cage. Wherever he touched Cory, Cory touched him, and Scott needed to feel more—more of Cory, more of Cory feeling him.

He pushed at the offending briefs, and Cory lifted up, helping to push them off, and dipped his hand down to Cory's groin. His fingers tangled in soft wiry curls before he closed them around Cory's erection. The first cock he'd ever held that wasn't his, and Christ Almighty, did he love the heavy feel of it in his palm. He groaned and rocked forward when his own straining cock was wrapped in a warm, firm grip, sliding slowly from base to head.

Cory pulled his leg out from between Scott's and hooked it over Scott's hip, tugging them closer, close enough for their cocks to bump heads, and the sensation sent a rush of adrenaline bouncing through his veins.

"Shit, Cory."

Those blue eyes met his and captured him, fully and completely. Cory hummed, lining their cocks up together and taking them both in his hand—his agile, brilliant, perfect hand—he began to stroke them as one.

Cory had him, literally and figuratively. Owned him. And Scott couldn't imagine anything better, anything he wanted more, anything he could ever want more.

Cory stroked them faster, Scott's body tightening as a powerful orgasm built to its inevitable release, and his eyes began to sting. A shout rose from the bottom of his lungs and echoed around them as his hot cum splashed between them. Cory joined him seconds later. Scott's throat constricted, and burning tears slid down his cheeks.

Scott threw an arm over his face. "Fuck." He didn't do tears. He didn't cry. Ever. But to do it right after that amazing experience with Cory . . .?

"Hey." Cory's voice was soft, compassionate, and the tears came tenfold.

"Sorry," Scott managed to croak. "This is embarrassing."

"No," Cory said, moving up and sliding a hand behind Scott's neck. "Let it go, Scott. You need to do this. Let it go."

He tried to force back the tears, tried to calm his racing heart, tried to say no, that he was good, but a sob escaped and that was it. The floodgates opened. He pulled Cory close, Cory's arms wrapped around him, holding him so he wouldn't break, and he buried his face in Cory's shoulder and cried.

He cried because for the first time in his life, sex felt right. For the first time, he knew he was with the person he was meant to be with.

He cried for all the years he'd hated himself and hated others like him. Cried for the people he'd hurt—emotionally and physically—because he wasn't strong enough to be who he was. He cried for all the years he'd wasted, all the opportunities he'd missed, for the father he never knew, and for a future that came with so much negative baggage. But most of all, he cried because Cory was an angel he never deserved and whose gentle acceptance and steadfast friendship had humbled him in ways he never could have imagined.

He cried until there was not another tear left to shed and exhaustion dragged him under.

CHAPTER SIXTEEN

Two hours later, Scott stepped out of the shower and looked in the mirror. This time he wasn't looking for the difference to show because he knew it *wouldn't* show there. Everything that was different was inside of him, and finally, for once in his life, that felt good. He could accept who he was now. He could move forward.

He toweled off quickly, stepped into a clean pair of jeans, and followed his nose downstairs. After he woke up from his embarrassing but incredibly relieving breakdown, Cory had offered to make him breakfast. Scott didn't know what he'd found in there to make, but whatever it was, it smelled like heaven.

"Hey, handsome," Cory said when Scott entered the kitchen. He strode across the room and pulled Cory into his arms, kissing him like it had been months instead of minutes since the last time. Then he let go, grinned when Cory swayed, and sat down at the island in the same chair Cory had been sitting in the night before. "Well, good morning to you too," Cory said, putting a hand over his heart.

"Smells good in here," Scott said.

"Cinnamon French toast."

"My favorite."

"I know. I found a recipe box in the cupboard and 'Scott's Fave' was written on it." Cory grinned, and it was so sheepishly adorable Scott couldn't help but smile in return. "I love your smile," Cory said and then clapped his hands together. "Food for my man, now!"

His man. Me. Scott searched for the old panic, for the familiar anger, the fight that had always lingered just below the surface anytime anything tried to make him see himself for who he was, but it wasn't there. Not even a hint in the background. Nothing. He was Cory's man, and surprisingly, a tiny little part of him wanted the whole world to know.

Eventually.

Cory served up breakfast with a flourish, earning not only a smile, but also laughter from Scott. And Christ, that felt good. He hadn't genuinely laughed in too long, hadn't felt genuinely good, and it was a welcome relief.

Halfway through breakfast, Cory put his fork down. "Can I ask you something?"

"Shoot." Scott shoved a mouthful of food into his mouth. Cory had to have added a secret family ingredient of his own to the recipe because he couldn't remember it tasting that good before. Maybe Cory would make them again for him some morning.

"You don't have to answer if you don't want to, of course, because I'm probably being too nosy and it's really none of my business, but . . ." He grabbed his knife and spun it around on the table a couple of times. "Why were you so angry? Before. Why did you hate yourself so much and go out of your way to be mean to people? Because I can't see that man at all."

"Thank you," Scott said and smiled. Or attempted to anyway. He didn't really care to get into all his dirty laundry, and the only person who knew everything was Brandi. But for some odd reason, he wanted Cory to know.

Scott put his utensils down and leaned back in his chair, taking a breath. "My dad was gay."

Cory's eyebrows shot up to his hairline. "What?"

Scott grinned. "Didn't expect that one, did you?"

Cory shook his head, eyes still wide, and rolled his hand rapidly in a hurry-up-and-continue gesture.

"Before I had any real inkling that I was different from the other boys at school, my mom and dad split up. My mom told me my dad left her—left *us*—for another man because he was gay. I didn't know what gay meant at the time, but I remember thinking it had to be some terrible thing. The divorce did my mom in. She started drinking, money got tight, the house was foreclosed, and we did a stint in shelters. All the while, she blamed every single bad thing in our lives on my dad."

Scott looked down at his plate, and the food he'd just eaten did a little backflip in the bottom of his stomach. Nothing like a little guilt to turn everything upside down.

"It wasn't all his fault, though, was it?"

Scott shook his head. "But I believed every word she said. I was too young to question anything. My parents were still gods to me then. Anyway, her hate ignited mine. I hated my dad, hated that he was gay, hated anything and everything gay from that moment on, because *gay* destroyed my family. And then when I realized that I might be . . . the same way, I fought it tooth and nail." Scott huffed a mirthless laugh. "Even checked myself into a gay conversion therapy center. They promised to make me straight, but they lied. They couldn't fix me, so my anger and self-hate only grew. Want to hear something crazy?"

Cory nodded, leaning forward on the countertop, fully engrossed in Scott's sordid tale.

"Tripp's dad owned the center I went to."

"No way!"

Scott nodded. "That's why I originally started bull riding. I needed to find the most hypermasculine sport I could to prove I was a *real* man. What a fucking stupid asshole I was."

Cory reached across the counter and placed his hand over Scott's. "Don't do that. You're not that guy anymore."

Scott turned his hand so their palms faced and laced their fingers. Cory gave a small squeeze of support.

"So . . . it was much later, when my mom ended up in the hospital with liver disease from all the drinking, that I found out the truth. I honestly don't think I have a single memory of her without a drink in her hand before then. Anyway, finally sober but with not much of a life left to live, she felt it was time to come clean. Apparently, what had made our lives hell was her addiction to the bottle and her own anger at learning her husband not only wanted a divorce but wanted it to pursue a relationship with a man.

"Dad had actually sent money every month to help support me, but she drank it all. He'd tried to see me, but Mom wouldn't let him have any contact with me at all—afraid he'd somehow turn me gay." Scott grinned at the irony. "But it was too little, too late. The damage had been done."

"That's why you got so upset the night we went to dinner and Harlan was there with Tanner."

Scott nodded. "Yeah. It brought back all that old anger, and I automatically painted Harlan the same as my dad. But I know that's not true now."

"So not what I was expecting to hear," Cory said. "Did you ever try to track your dad down then? After you learned the truth?"

Scott shook his head. "Too many years and too much water under the bridge."

"How long has it been since you talked to him?"

Scott huffed and then looked away, hoping Cory didn't see the flash of regret he knew had reached his eyes. "I haven't seen or talked to him since I was fourteen years old."

Cory nodded. "I think maybe it's time you do something about mending that bridge."

CHAPTER SEVENTEEN

"I got him!" Tanner shouted, the glee in his voice infectious. "Did you see that, Scott?"

"I sure did." Scott held up a hand to give Tanner a high five when Tanner and Harlan rode back to the roping stalls. "Way to go, buddy."

It was early morning, a few hours until the rodeo got underway, and Harlan was practicing team roping with Tanner—a much safer sport for a nine-year-old. Scott was helping by running steers through to the roping chutes, and Cory was hazing the cattle from the arena.

Tanner backed his horse into the stall on the left, which meant he'd be the header—roping the steer's horns—and Harlan, backing into the right stall, was the heeler, and his was the harder job, roping the hind legs. Scott got the steer ready to set free and waited for Harlan's cue to open the gate.

"Tighten your honda a little more, Tan," Harlan said over the cattle chute between the two stalls. "Yep, like that. Remember, you want to already be swinging your lasso when the steer is set loose. You should be ready to throw your coils in three swings or less."

"I got it, Dad," Tanner said like a kid who'd heard it a million times.

Scott grinned. Tanner did have it. So far he'd only missed one toss out of five. Not bad at all. Scott looked over at Harlan, who nodded, and Scott pulled the chute doors open.

Harlan's and Tanner's horses bolted from the stalls at a gallop, at the same time the steer made a run for it. Tanner swung his lasso five times before he threw his coils, and Scott thought for sure he was going to miss this time. They were almost out of arena. But Tanner managed to catch his rope around the steer's horns and quickly turned him so Harlan could throw his coils and . . . miss.

"Aw, bummer," Tanner said. "Better luck next time."

Harlan laughed, and a sharp pang of jealousy startled Scott.

This was what he'd missed out on with his dad: the bonding over activities and hobbies they both enjoyed together, his father teaching him new things. But maybe he could have some of that now. If he reached out.

"Can we go one more time?" Tanner asked when Harlan dismounted to free the steer of Tanner's rope. "Please?"

The steer didn't know which way to go, but Cory rode up alongside it, guiding it toward the exit gate on the other side of the arena.

"Just one more," Harlan said, climbing up into his saddle. "Then we gotta clear the ring."

"And then we get pancakes, right?"

Harlan laughed while they coiled their ropes as they returned to the stalls.

"You got it, Tan."

Tanner hooted as they backed their horses into the stalls again, while Scott got another steer ready. Harlan nodded, Scott released the steer, and this time Tanner and Harlan both had accurate throws, capturing their steer in mere seconds. The two were going to make a good roping team, if Tanner stuck with it.

Scott turned away, focusing on getting the chute ready for the next steers to come through when the rodeo officially got underway. He and his dad had already missed too many years together. Even though he didn't know his dad's side of the story, he had an idea now of what it must have been like for him. Scott had had enough trouble—still did—coming to terms with himself, but he could only imagine how hard it must have been for his dad. Scott didn't know if it was possible at this point, but just maybe he and his own dad could start again.

Scott watched Harlan and Tanner ride out of the arena, side by side. Harlan leaned over in his saddle, reaching out a hand and dropping it on Tanner's shoulder. Tanner smiled and nodded in response to whatever Harlan had said. That's how it should be, fathers and sons. Brandi and Cory were right. It was time. He was ready.

Scott turned to find Cory watching him from his horse a few feet away. "You looked a million miles away just now," Cory said.

Scott walked over to stand at the horse's shoulder and ran a hand along his thick neck. He stared up at Cory, those gorgeous blue eyes gazing back. "Would you help me find my dad?"

Cory beamed. "Absolutely."

"Do you have any idea where to start?" Cory asked before taking a bite of his apple.

Scott sat beside him in a foldable chair in front of Cory's trailer. Once he'd decided he wanted to find his dad, it had been all he could think about. As soon as the rodeo wrapped and they'd finished cleaning that day, they'd gone straight to Cory's campsite to figure out what to do next. "California somewhere," Scott said. "I think."

Cory eyed him. "California is kind of a big state."

"Before my mom passed, she gave me my dad's last known address," Scott said. The day she'd confessed how her hurt and anger had estranged him and his father, and as a result, changed the course of his life in a very negative way. How different would both of their lives have been if she'd just been honest from the start? "But it's probably in a box in my storage locker, where I'd put everything nonessential when I moved to Brandi's."

"Where's your locker?"

"Stockton." Scott got up and dug a cola out of the cooler beside the trailer. "But I have no idea which box, if I even kept the address."

"I'm the Google-fu ninja, remember?" Cory leaned half-out of his chair and pulled his phone from his back pocket. He wiggled it at Scott. "I will find him."

Scott laughed but didn't doubt Cory would do just that.

"Name, please?"

For a second, Scott couldn't remember. For so many years, he'd ignored the fact that his dad even existed. "Darren. Darren Gillard," he said, and a mix of apprehension and anticipation bled through him. That name was so far removed from him but belonged to the one person who'd had the biggest impact on his life. He turned his attention to Cory's nimble fingers tapping away on the phone screen.

"Bingo!" Cory crowed a few minutes later. "Found three Darren Gillards: Hesperia, Rancho Cucamonga, and San Leandro. How much do I rock?"

Scott grinned. "Much."

Cory flashed a coy, sideways look at him and waved him off with a smile. "Which one do you want to call first?"

"Call?" Scott gulped, and then Cory's hand was on his thigh.

"I'll be right here," Cory said, that sweet voice as magically soothing to Scott's ears as the hand resting on his leg. "And if you want to go meet him, I'd also be happy to go with you."

"Thank you," Scott said. Knowing Cory was there and would be with him made it that much easier to follow through. "Let's, uh . . . let's start with the closest, San Leandro. Maybe we'll get lucky."

Cory squeezed his thigh before removing his hand and tapping on the phone again. Then he handed the phone to Scott, who stared at it like the thing had fangs and might bite him. *Stop being a baby.*

He grabbed the phone and held it to his ear—and also held his breath. Just as he was about to hang up, the line connected. He didn't recognize the voice of the man who answered, but then wondered why he thought he would.

"Hello, uh . . ." Scott looked over at Cory, who smiled and urged him on with a nod of his head. "I'm looking for a Darren Gillard."

"This is Darren," the man, possibly his dad, said.

"Is this the same Darren Gillard who was married to a woman named Judith and had a son named Scott?"

A sucked-in breath echoed down the line, and silence followed. "Scott?"

Scott closed his eyes and his voice cracked when he said, "Hi, Dad."

CHAPTER EIGHTEEN

Three days later, Scott stood on the front porch of an immaculately cared for California bungalow, more nervous than the moment before the gate opened for his very first bull ride. Beside him, Cory looped their pinky fingers and gave a little squeeze, smiling up at him, and the nerves eased a little. That Cory had come with him to meet his dad and his dad's husband meant more to him than he could find the words to express.

Then the front door opened, and an older version of himself stood on the other side of the threshold. The nerves he'd just managed to rein in stampeded off again.

"Scott." His father's voice was softer than he remembered, but then, maybe he was nervous too. "Please, come in."

Scott glanced at Cory, who smiled and gave him a nudge, and the two of them followed his dad into a welcoming living room. Scott wasn't usually one for noticing decor, but the furnishings in this house were tasteful and masculine while not being overly so, and earth tones enhanced the sense of comfort. Under any other circumstance, he'd have felt quite relaxed, but not today, not in this situation. Right now he felt all kinds of uncomfortable while they all stood in the middle of the room. What was he supposed to say? How was he supposed to act? Maybe this really wasn't the best idea and he should just leave.

A man entered the room through a wide archway, carrying a tray with a pitcher of iced tea on it and four glasses. He was tall, willowy, but his eyes held a glow to them that told Scott this was the kind of person who'd give his last dollar to a stranger in need.

"Scott," his dad said, "this is Cal, my husband." Cal stepped forward, his smile wide and genuine, and offered his hand, which Scott accepted automatically. "Cal, this is Scott. My son."

"Such a pleasure to finally met you, Scott," Cal said. He shifted his attention to Cory; curiosity in his eyes while waiting for an introduction.

"I'm sorry," Scott said, feeling his cheeks heat. "This is Cory, my . . ." Fuck, what did he say? Boyfriend? That sounded . . . strange. Somehow not quite right. It wasn't the concept of Cory being his boyfriend that tangled him up as much as the word itself. How could he claim Cory was his boyfriend to anyone when he couldn't show it?

His dad and Cal shared a quick look, but they seemed happy enough to leave the introduction hanging. Cal shook Cory's hand, and then his dad turned to Cory. "It's a pleasure to meet you, Cory. I'm Darren."

"So wonderful to meet you both," Cory said.

Scott's dad and Cal shared another glance, the kind of silent communication only couples who'd been together forever seemed to develop. "Say, Cory," Cal said, "would you mind helping me in the kitchen for a minute?"

Cory looked to Scott first, and as much as he didn't want to be alone with his dad, he knew it was probably best. He smiled at Cory, a halfhearted, resigned lift of his lips, he knew, but Cory seemed to understand. All the confidence Scott needed shone back at him from that peaceful blue gaze. Cory moved like he was going to reach out to him in some way, hug him maybe, but then changed his mind, and with a quick smile and brief nod, he followed Cal out of the room.

And now that he was alone with his father, Scott's discomfort amped up tenfold.

"Please, have a seat." His dad gestured to the couch sitting in front of a large bay window, and Scott sat. It was comfortable, yet *not.*

His father sat across from him on a matching recliner, but it seemed they both were at a loss at how to start or what to say now that their respective other halves had left the room. And Cory was his other half, wasn't he? Even though Scott hadn't been able to say, *I'm gay, and he's my boyfriend*, he knew it was true.

"I hated you," Scott finally said, and his dad visibly jerked back. He was aware that probably wasn't the best way to start a reunion, but it was out there now, and just as good a place to start as any: with the truth.

"I'm so sorry, Scott," his dad said, staring down at his hands for a second. "I didn't want to hurt anyone, and I tried for years to reach you."

"I know." Scott sighed, and his dad's eyes met his, hope dancing in dark depths that looked so much like his own. "I know now. A couple of years ago, Mom finally told me the truth, before she passed away, but up until then, I hated you and everything that I associated with you." Scott swallowed the lump in his throat. "Including myself."

"Oh, Scott. I never wanted any of that. I . . . had been living a lie so long. I couldn't go on like that anymore. It was killing me, hurting your mom, hurting you. I needed to be strong, be myself, for the people I loved. And I did love your mother. Not the same way I love Cal, but I only wanted her, and you, to be happy. I'd hoped my coming out would have given her the freedom to find someone who could love her fully, like she deserved."

"But she lost her life in a bottle instead, and I . . ." Scott's throat tightened, choking off his words. He stared at the doorway Cory had gone through, willing him to come back, willing him to share some of his light and strength so Scott could get through this. "I have an idea . . . how hard it must have been trying to be someone you weren't."

His dad talked of that time, shared his experience in coming to terms with himself and coming out, but Scott found himself zoning out. He'd hated his dad for so long, and that hate had set his life on a destructive course. And then to discover all those years later that everything he'd believed was a lie. He wouldn't hate his mother for it, though. She'd suffered through enough of her own pain, right up to her last breath.

If only his dad had tried harder, or his mom hadn't gone so far off the deep end, then things would be different today. But then he may not have been compelled to throw himself into one of the most dangerous sports he could find. Might not have met Cory.

"I can see a lot of myself in you, Scott," his father was saying as Scott tried to pick up the thread of their conversation. "I can't tell you how many times I'd wished things could have been different, that I could have been there to help you when you needed my support the most."

Tears pricked at his eyes. *Jesus Christ, what the fuck is wrong with me and the fucking crying lately?* "My life would have been completely different," he said, hoping his voice sounded steadier than it felt.

"I hope your life hasn't been very bad."

Only as bad as I made it. Scott shook his head and glanced at the empty doorway again. His dad didn't need to know; he'd had enough of his own bad, and Scott wasn't about to add old bad to it now. Not when he'd been walking in both shoes.

"He's more than just a friend, isn't he?" His dad's voice was quiet, gentle, and Scott suddenly wanted to tell him everything. Instead, he shrugged. Maybe one day, if there were more days he would get to spend with his dad after this one.

Cory and Cal came around the corner then, Cal laughing while Cory speed-talked, his hands fluttering along, accenting his words. And just like that, the weight and confusion that had started pressing in on him lifted.

"Does he ever stop?" Cal asked, sitting on the arm of the chair his dad sat in.

Scott couldn't help the smile that pulled at his mouth. "Eventually, yes."

"This house is so gorgeous," Cory said, sitting down beside him. "You need to get Darren to take you for a tour. Oh my God. And you have got to see the bathroom! It's like a full-on spa in there, with a Jacuzzi tub and three rain heads in the shower. And the backyard is like some kind of private oasis. I could so see myself living in a house like this."

Scott took in the surroundings again, but this time he saw his dad and Cal in the house. They were part of the comfort that permeated the space around them. Scott watched them: Cal with an arm draped over the back of the chair, tangling a finger in his dad's hair. His dad leaning into Cal, looking up at his husband with one of the warmest, most loving smiles Scott had ever seen. His dad reached for Cal's free hand, brought it to his mouth and kissed its palm before twining their fingers together. Then, as if realizing they were being watched, they both turned toward Scott and smiled. They were utterly content, utterly in love.

And that's when it hit him.

This wasn't just a house, it was a *home*. Love lived in every corner of it, and it lived loud and proud. Suddenly that feeling of comfort became suffocating. He needed to get out. Needed to run away from them, from himself . . . from Cory, who wanted a life like this. How could he ever live this way? The picket fence and the dog and the two-point-one kids and the minivan. Like his dad and Cal did. Scott had noticed signs of a dog but didn't see a minivan. Didn't mean there wasn't one in the garage.

This wasn't the kind of life he could give Cory.

But you could.

No. Cory needed, deserved, someone better, someone stronger, someone who could finish his sentences and would share the paper over breakfast and hang photos of their life together on the walls. Someone out and proud and not afraid to show affection in public.

You can *be that person. You* can *do all those things.*

No. I can't.

Scott stood up abruptly, and three pairs of eyes looked at him expectantly. His pulse raced, and his feet twitched with the need to flee. "I . . . uh. I need to go. Now. Sorry."

"Oh. Yes. I guess it's getting late," his dad said as everyone rose, and Scott ignored the twinge of guilt at the note of disappointment in his father's voice. "Thank you for reaching out to me, son. I very much hope we'll get to spend more time together."

Son.

"I'd like that," Scott managed, swallowing back the avalanche of emotions that crashed into him at every angle. He extended his hand, intending a quick handshake so he wouldn't be too rude, but his dad hugged him instead. It was short, awkward, and a little piece of the kid he used to be mourned for the years he'd lost with his father. They both cleared their throats when they stepped back, and then Cal was shaking his hand, saying how good it was to meet him and Cory, and that hopefully they'd all get to visit again soon. Scott nodded in all the right places until he could run for the door without looking like he was bolting.

"Are you okay?" Cory asked when they pulled away from the street, out of suburbia, and back toward the kind of life Scott knew how to live.

"Yep. Good," he said without even a sideways glance. He couldn't handle those caring, promising eyes right now. Eyes that made him believe he could be a better person, that he could live out in the open. With Cory.

"Mind if I don't believe you?"

Scott looked for traffic both ways and then turned onto the main road. He shrugged. "You're entitled to your opinion."

"What just happened there, Scott?"

God, the way Cory said his name, like he was something special, someone worth having, only illustrated how much he really wasn't.

"Not right now." His emotions were too high, his skin felt raw, peeled back, and he knew if Cory pushed him, he'd say something he'd regret.

"I'm just worried," Cory continued as if he hadn't heard. "Something doesn't feel right here and—"

"Stop." *Please, Cory. Don't push me.* "I can't do this right now."

"Can't do what?" Cory's voice rose on the last word, and the spinning wheel of Scott's emotions landed on anger.

Scott slammed on the brakes and steered the truck hard to curb. Throwing it into park, he rounded on Cory. "This! I can't do this. I can't have this talk right now. I can't live like they do. I can't give you any of that. I'm not that kind of man. Fuck, Cory! I'm not the right guy for someone like yo—"

"Don't you dare throw this back on me." The hard snap in Cory's voice took him aback. "This isn't about not being good enough for me so you're going to be the big martyr and let me go to find someone who is. *Oh no.* This is about you being terrified of anyone finding out you're gay."

"No. That's not true," Scott said, but the words felt like the lie they were as they slid off his tongue. "You know I'm working my way there."

"Really?" Cory waved a hand in the air. "Because we just spent over an hour with two men you should have been able to be completely open and honest with."

"I don't know them," Scott tried to reason, only realizing how lame that sounded after the words echoed back to him. Some of the fight drained out of him while it seemed to be growing in Cory.

"He's your *father*," Cory bit out. "Of all the people you know, he's the one who has been in your shoes. He could help you learn to deal with it so you can live a full life."

Cory snapped off his seat belt and yanked on the door handle.

"Where are you going?"

"Home!" Cory jumped from the cab and a blast of fear chilled the last remnants of anger in Scott's body.

"Cory—"

"You couldn't even introduce me to them. I didn't expect you to come right out and say, 'This is my boyfriend,' but you couldn't even acknowledge me as a friend. It's like you were embarrassed to have me there."

"That's not true. I wanted you there." Scott fought squirming in his seat. "And . . . I told my dad."

Cory paused, holding on to the door but not closing it; whatever his next words were, they stalled, and both of his eyebrows lifted. "What did you say?"

"I don't remember," Scott lied.

"Did you say, 'Dad, Cory's my boyfriend'? Did you say those words?"

"No!" Scott's anger perked back up. Couldn't Cory just let it go so he could calm down and collect his thoughts? "He asked if you were more than a friend. That was it."

"And your response?"

Scott stared at his hands on the steering wheel. He whispered, "I shrugged."

Silence stretched between them. Only the steady rumbling idle of the truck and a dog barking somewhere in the distance registered to Scott. And then Cory sighed.

"I really thought we could be something." Cory's voice was softer now, a note of sadness in it triggered a wave of panic in Scott's chest. He was going to lose Cory. Right now, if he didn't figure out how to fix this in the next two seconds.

"But not if it's only in private where no one can see or know," Cory said.

"No. Cory, please. Don't quit me." Scott didn't care that his voice was almost a whine. "Get back in the truck. Let me drive you home."

"I can get home all by myself, thank you very much. Besides, if people see us together, they might get the wrong idea and think you're gay. We can't have that. So, don't you worry about me. Go live your life your way, and I'll go live mine my way. Deal?"

The door slammed on Scott's "No," leaving him sitting there alone—chest heaving, skin crawling and clammy, and a sickening lurch in his stomach. "No deal."

How the fuck did that get so out of hand?

CHAPTER NINETEEN

The lights flicked on, and Scott blinked as his eyes adjusted to the sudden brightness.

"Oh no." Brandi dropped her purse on the floor and crossed the living room to sit on the coffee table in front of him. "What happened?"

He'd been sitting on the couch nursing the same beer for so long the sun had given way to darkness while he'd been staring out the window seeing nothing. He couldn't even remember what he'd been thinking, only knew that his mind was a mess after the meeting with his dad and Cory walking out on him.

Brandi pried the bottle from his hand and made a face. "Please tell me you're not drinking hot beer." She put the bottle on the table beside her and took his hand in hers.

"No." Scott frowned and looked down at their joined hands. "Just holding on, I guess." And he almost laughed at how not literal that was.

Giving his hand a squeeze before letting go, she gathered his beer bottle and disappeared into the kitchen. Clinking glass and running water echoed through the otherwise quiet house. What seemed like only seconds later, she was back on her perch on the coffee table, pushing an ice-cold glass of water into his hand.

"Drink and then tell me what happened." She leaned forward, elbows on her knees, hands clasped.

He drank half the glass before stopping to breathe, the cold liquid quenching the parched corners of his throat. Then he gave her a rundown of the day. How Cory had gone with him, but when it came to introductions he'd frozen on what to call Cory. How his father's house had been such a *home*. How he'd freaked, and the worst part of it all, the light in Cory's eyes going out as he'd slammed the truck door and walked away.

Brandi studied him for a long moment, then sat up. "Tell me about your dad."

She never went for the obvious when she had her therapist hat on but worked toward it in a roundabout way that let him discover the lightbulb moment more profoundly. "Looks like me, only older and a couple of inches taller, leaner. He's a graphic designer—does movie posters for the big studios mostly. He was . . . not what I expected."

"What did you expect?"

He shrugged. "Not sure really. I think I expected to hate him on sight, but I . . . liked him."

"And his husband?"

"Cal," Scott said. "Good Samaritan type. He took Cory for a tour around the house while Dad and I talked. Something about the fact that Cal's the one Dad left us for is a comfort. I couldn't find a reason to resent either of them for it."

"Because he left to be with the person he was meant to be with, not just to be a footloose and fancy-free playboy?"

He stared into his glass. Light filtered through the melting ice cubes, rainbow tinting their smooth corners. "I guess." He took another deep swallow.

"You said the house was a home. What was the difference?"

Scott thought for a moment. It felt lived in, comfortable, and welcoming, but most of all . . . "It was them. They made it a home."

"Why do you think that freaked you out?"

"I don't know. It was just all so . . . committed. Domestic. *Normal.*" He huffed a halfhearted laugh. "I have a small rancher on thirty acres, and the barn is always cleaner and more organized than the house. More lived in. I only know that and the road. Then looking at me, Cory said he could live in a home like Dad and Cal's, and it just felt like . . . I don't know. Like I was supposed to agree or something."

Brandi crossed her legs, lacing her fingers together to cup her knee. "I have a theory."

He searched her eyes for a second and only found patience and compassion in them. Sometimes there was a question or concern there, and those times he really didn't want to hear what she had to say. "Go on."

"I think perhaps your dad's house represents everything you didn't have growing up—the safety and security of a loving, committed family, a place of permanence, a place you know you can be you, unconditionally. That not only scared you, but you somehow associated that with coming out. That you can't have a home unless you do."

"That doesn't make sense."

"No? For a lot of people, getting what they really want most scares them so much they subconsciously sabotage their chances of ever reaching it. Let's say, hypothetically, you wanted to build a home with Cory, but that scares you because then you'd have something you could lose. You already lost it once before, when your dad left. So, logical or not, if you never come out, you'll never have to worry about giving yourself over to someone or something that would hurt you to lose. Plus, Cory can't be anything but out and proud, and you said yourself a while ago, that people will automatically assume you're gay too, just because you're with him. So, basically, Cory and your dad represent everything you want but are afraid to reach for."

Scott shook his head. It made sense in a weird way. "I'm a mess, aren't I?"

She smiled and cupped his cheek. "Not at all. You just need to learn to listen to the quiet voice in your head. It's smarter than the loud one. Trust that voice, and you'll find your way."

"Mind if I join you guys for a hand?"

The gay circuit was out of state the weekend following his blowout with Cory, so Scott had been working with Tripp on a pro tour stop in Chico. He'd hoped Cory would be there, but the only pickup riders on the scene were Marty and Bridge. Since Chico was a six-hour drive round trip, he'd decided to camp out on the rodeo grounds for the weekend. The day's events were done, but Scott didn't want to spend the night sitting in his camper by himself. That just gave him too much time to think about how he'd fucked up with Cory.

"Sorry, man. Table's kind of full right now," Kent said, but there was no animosity or malice in his voice. He was just stating a fact that Scott could clearly see himself.

"Here. You can take my seat." One of the cowboys Scott had seen around for years but whose name he never knew, tossed his cards in the middle of the table with a dejected huff. "I'm out."

Scott looked to Kent and Bridge to make sure it was okay. While he'd never hung out with them, he knew these poker games were their baby. Kent's attention was on the cards he was shuffling, but Bridge met Scott's gaze. He kicked out the now-empty chair and said, "Five-buck buy-in."

"Thank you," he said. Not all that long ago, Bridge would have told him where to go and what he could do when he got there.

Scott settled into the chair and pulled a five-dollar bill from his wallet. He glanced around the table. In addition to Bridge and Kent, Tripp, Roy, and a cowboy named John he'd never met before were playing. Marty and Eric sat in camping chairs talking with a couple of cowboys and a woman. The only one missing was Cory.

Scott swallowed down his longing and gathered the cards as Kent dealt them out.

"Where's your boy this weekend?" Roy asked, eyes on sorting the cards in his hand.

"He's not—" *My boy*. But Scott wanted him to be. Though Cory was no boy. He was a strong, proud man, and fuck, Scott wished he were there right now. But for that to happen, he had to grab some balls and cowboy up. His throat suddenly felt dry and the palms of his hands clammy, but he ventured out onto the metaphorical ledge. "He's doing his own thing, I guess."

"He's a nice kid," Roy said, still not looking up from his hand. He tapped the table, and Kent dealt him a card.

That was it? Scott glanced at John, who was also focused on his cards. Scott rubbed his hand on his jeans. Roy had basically just outed him and no one even blinked. Except Bridge, who wasn't blinking at all, and Scott fought the urge to squirm under the intense stare.

"I'm sorry," Bridge said. "Did I miss something here, because what the fuck?"

"Not now," Tripp said. The clear warning in his voice drew a curious look from Roy; John remained oblivious. Bridge shot a surprised scowl at Tripp before pursing his lips. Then he turned back to Scott. "That young man is like a little brother to me. Understand?"

Scott nodded. "Got it." He definitely understood the message loud and clear. He'd have issued the same one.

The warning lingered in Bridge's eyes, and then he shook his head and picked up his beer. He frowned before tossing it into a box of empties behind him. "Babe," he called to Eric. "Can you toss me a brew?"

Instead of tossing, Eric brought it over and planted a kiss on Bridge's cheek. "Thank you," Bridge said, smiling.

Scott tracked Eric as he went back to his chair. The other three people were still there, and one of the cowboys was holding the woman's hand. Two gay couples on the pro rodeo circuit, hanging out with straight cowboys, and not a one of them cast a sideways glance or made a derogatory comment.

A clash of emotions banged around inside his head, his heart, his gut—surprise, anger, regret, envy, longing, hope, and most of all an emptiness where Cory had been. He scanned the table and campsite again. Tripp, Marty, Bridge, Eric . . . all confident and secure in who they were and in their relationships. They didn't back down. They didn't apologize. They were all proud, strong, incredible men. Men to admire and look up to.

And then there was him. He used to think he was strong, but he never had been. He'd been nothing but a coward hiding behind stupid words and quick fists. What the hell was he so afraid of when these guys had unknowingly already paved the way for him?

Fuck, I miss Cory.

So what are you going to do about it?

Get him back.

The phone in his jeans pocket rang, and he jumped up from the table, drawing five pairs of surprised eyes. "Sorry. I gotta get this." He dropped his cards on the table. "I fold," he said. Which sucked because he was holding a straight flush, but who might be on the phone was more important than winning a few bucks.

He stepped away and answered without looking at the caller ID, hoping against hope it was Cory. He'd been calling Cory ever since their argument earlier in the week, but every call had gone straight to voice mail and not a single one was returned.

"Hello?" He couldn't control the eagerness in his voice.

"Hi, Scott." The voice on the other end sounded vaguely familiar, but it wasn't Cory's. The light that had sparked inside faded. "It's, uh . . . Darren."

"Oh. Hi, Dad," Scott said, walking around to the other side of Marty's equine rig, where he sat on the tire well.

There was a long pause and then, "Expecting someone else?"

Something Cory had said during their fight came to mind, about how his dad probably would be the best person for him to talk to, to help him. He wanted Cory back, he wanted a relationship with his dad, but in order to have both, he'd have to take the first step. "Hoping," he said. "I was hoping it would be Cory."

"Is everything okay?" The concern in his dad's voice was genuine, and Scott told him everything that had happened after they left his house last week.

"I know we've only just reconnected," his dad said, "and I really have no right to ask this, but . . . can I offer a little fatherly advice?"

"Yes. Please." *Tell me what to do.*

"If you truly care about Cory and want him in your life—"

"I do!"

"Then don't let your fears keep you from the one you're meant to spend your life with. My own fears almost cost me Cal. He'd promised to wait for me, but I took advantage of that so I wouldn't have to make a decision, and slowly he began to drift away. It was when I saw him at a club talking to another man—laughing and smiling, more relaxed than I'd seen in months—that I realized he wasn't happy, and I was losing him."

"That's when you came out?" Scott took off his hat, holding it in his lap as he leaned back and let his head rest against the smooth metal of the trailer.

"Yes, and it was almost too late. Don't wait that long, son."

"I don't know what to do." Scott sighed. It all sounded so simple. "He won't answer my calls."

"Then it's time for the grand gesture."

Chapter Twenty

Cory stared at the caller ID on his phone and almost answered, but he tossed the phone onto his bed. More than a week had passed since that fateful visit with Scott's dad, and the hurt and anger still lingered. Scott had called him every single day since, sometimes twice a day. At first Cory was too indignant to answer because, even though Scott said over and over how much he was trying, when confronted in any way, he turned and ran from the truth.

When the anger began to retreat, guilt slipped in. Scott had warned him that he might stumble backward occasionally and had asked Cory to have patience with him. But he hadn't. Scott stumbled, and instead of giving him a little space to process, Cory had gone on the offensive, pushed him into a fight, and then dumped him.

Now he didn't know what to do. He missed Scott, missed his dry humor and the way he blushed and the taste of his mouth. But he knew himself well enough to know he wouldn't be able to date a closeted man. Not for long. The lack of an introduction at Scott's dad's house had hurt in more ways than he could express.

He reached for his phone and pressed Marty's number.

"I need help," Cory said by way of a greeting when Marty answered. "Did you know Scott and I were kind of seeing each other?"

Silence on the other end. Not even breathing rattled the line. "Scott Gillard?"

"Yes, and—"

"Cory, he's—"

"Don't!" Cory rolled over and stared up at the ceiling. "He's not the same guy you knew before."

"Okay," Marty finally said.

"The problem is he's closeted, and I'm not. I know that I couldn't ever handle a relationship like that, but I miss him so much."

Marty was quiet for a long minute. "Did you know Tripp and I had split up before he came out?"

Cory shook his head and then realized Marty couldn't see him. "No. I don't know anything about your love story."

Marty chuckled. "I like that. Our 'love story' was a bit rough, though. After dating in secret for over a year, I finally realized Tripp was never going to come out. I couldn't force him, of course, but I couldn't live that way anymore. It was killing me, so I broke it off. It was one of the hardest things I'd ever done, but it was the right thing."

"How'd Tripp take it?" Cory flipped over onto his stomach and rested on his elbows.

"Not so good. But I was still there for him. I made sure he knew I'd be there to help him if he needed, but only as a friend.

"Your circumstances are unique to you, and only you can decide what's best for you, but if you really miss him, don't cut him from your life completely. Be there for him . . . as a friend. He may never come out, but he could. If I had cut Tripp out completely, he might never have left his closet, and we might never have had a chance for what we have now. And I wouldn't change that for the world."

"So you're saying?"

"I'm saying call him back and leave the door open."

"Okay," Cory said and sat up. He'd call right now, though he had no idea what he was going to say. "Thank you, Marty."

"Anytime," Marty said. "And let me know what happens. I want to hear your love story too."

Cory laughed and then disconnected. He stood up and paced his bedroom, finger hovering over Scott's number.

The doorbell rang downstairs, but it sounded miles away. The distant sound of less-than-friendly male voices drifted upstairs; one he knew was Toby's and the other sounded familiar enough to make his pulse kick up a notch. Then his name was shouted. Scott's voice—deep, gravelly, and panicked.

Cory's heart leaped in his chest, and he jumped up from his bed.

He'd been mad. He hadn't wanted to talk to Scott at all, but now that he'd had time to cool off and reflect, and talked to Marty, he had to at least listen to what Scott had to say. Hearing that sexy voice again, he couldn't get downstairs fast enough. He knew he had to rein himself in, though. He couldn't just charge down there and jump into Scott's arms like nothing had happened and things would be perfect from here on out. He couldn't be in an unbalanced relationship. No matter how much he wanted to be with Scott, they'd just have to stick to being friends.

The door was partway open when Cory entered the foyer, and he noticed the toe of Scott's boot blocking the jam while Toby warned him to leave.

Cory walked up behind Toby, so he could see Scott, and his heart triple-timed when their gazes met. Scott's eyes lit up, and relief spread across his handsome face. "Cory," he said, his voice an awestruck whisper. He took off his hat, holding it with both hands, and smiled. The kind of smile Cory had tried coaxing out of him more often, and suddenly he had trouble remembering why he couldn't get involved any deeper with Scott right now.

"Cory, please believe me when I say how very sorry I am for the way I acted at my dad's. I freaked, I know, but I swear to you that's not going to happen again. Ever."

That's why. Closets.

"How can I believe that? You can't even admit you're gay," Cory said. "What kind of relationship could we ever have like that? I can't do that, and it's not fair of you to expect it of me. It's also not fair of me to expect you to come out before you're ready, so like I said before, maybe now isn't our time."

"Cory, can you please come out here and talk to me?"

Cory shook his ahead. "I don't think it's a good idea right now. We need some time and space to get some perspective and figure out what we really want."

"I already got perspective, and I know what I want," Scott said, low and forceful. "It's you."

God, I want you, too. "It's not our time yet." Cory took a step back. "Please go."

"Cory, please," Scott said.

Cory turned and made for the stairs, but Toby's voice stopped him. His brother wasn't berating Scott, wasn't yelling at him like he had been since the moment they met.

"I'm sorry, Scott," Toby was saying, his voice genuinely apologetic.

"This was supposed to be my grand gesture to win him back," Scott said, his tone defeated, confused, and Cory's heart melted a little. What was he doing walking away from that man? Why couldn't he help Scott out of the closet from the inside? *Because that could be years. If ever.*

Toby laughed. "I haven't seen anything grand yet." He nudged Scott's boot out of the way and quietly closed the door. Toby turned and jumped when he saw Cory still standing here, obviously having expected him to have gone back upstairs already.

"Where's my brother?"

Toby's grin was self-effacing. "I had a long talk with Tripp. I might have been a little too harsh on Scott. And . . . I realized you're an adult and don't need me looking after you like some mother hen."

Cory's throat tightened. He wanted to run out the door and call Scott back, but he gave Toby a quick hug and then started up the stairs. "I'm hopping in the shower, then let's go out for some dinner."

Scott dropped his forehead to the smooth wood of the front door. Tears pricked at his eyes, a heavy weight pressed on his heart, but he was not leaving without a fight. Cory had gotten so far under his skin that somehow, when he hadn't been looking, not having Cory as a part of his life had become unacceptable.

Then it's time for the grand gesture. His dad's words echoed in his mind.

He stepped away from the door and stared up at the second-story windows.

"Cory Ackerson. I have something to tell you!" He kept backing up until he was standing on the sidewalk. He'd never actually been inside Cory's house before, so he had no idea which room was his. He'd just yell until Cory came out or he had no voice left. Then he'd start throwing rocks at the windows. But he was not leaving until he talked to Cory.

"Cory! Are you listening to me?"

A horn blared, a dog barked, and Scott glanced around. Last thing he needed was the neighbors calling the cops on him. Everything seemed pretty quiet, but two houses down, a woman poked her head up from the garden bed she'd obviously been working in.

"You might try the doorbell," she said.

Ha-ha. Brilliant. "He won't answer," Scott said.

The woman pushed her hat up and wiped her brow. "Well, carry on then."

Scott narrowed his eyes. Like he needed permission from the nosy neighbors. He refocused on the house and caught a flash of movement in the left window. A bright spark of hope lit in his mind, and he refocused his efforts on winning Cory back.

"I know you can hear me, so listen up." He walked closer to the house and onto the lawn under the window he hoped Cory was behind.

"I'm sorry for being an asshole. I'm sorry for not making you feel like the prince you are."

Nothing. He swallowed a few times, trying to lubricate his throat for continued abuse.

"Here's the really important part, Cory. You'd better be listening!"

Movement caught his eye, but it wasn't from the window. The gardening neighbor was now at his side, looking up at the window as he'd been. She glanced at Scott and motioned for him to continue. He stared at her in disbelief for a second, and shook his head.

Scott took a huge gulp of air and shouted as loud as he could. "I'm gay!"

"Congratulations!" someone yelled from the window of a passing car.

"I'm gay, Cory. Full-on, big-flaming-queen gay!"

A soft chuckle drifted up to his ears from his quiet cheerleader but still nothing from the window twenty feet above him. A cold ache slipped into his chest. Had he screwed up beyond all possible hope of repair? He'd never wanted to hurt Cory, vowed he wouldn't, but the old Scott just had to make an appearance. Wrapped him up so tight in his own mess that he couldn't see what it was doing to those around him. Never again. If he could just get Cory to come outside and talk to him, take him back, he'd never again let his crap get between them.

He had to keep trying.

"Cory Ackerson! I, Scott Gillard, am gay, and I'm head over heels in love with you!"

Fuck. Still nothing. The ache in his chest spread out, deepened.

"You hear me? I'm gay, and I'm in love with you!"

A hand gently gripped his forearm, and he looked down into a pair of shiny brown eyes. "He's coming," Garden Neighbor said softly and pointed at the door.

"I'm not so sure." Scott's voice cracked, hoarse from the yelling, but he would keep yelling until he couldn't make another sound. But he didn't have to. The door opened, and there stood Cory. Wet, messy hair, like he'd just washed it, sweatpants, and tears trickling down his cheeks, but he was the most beautiful thing Scott had ever laid eyes on. Hope rose in his chest, casting light back into a slowly darkening day.

"Hi, Mrs. Lu," Cory said, his voice shaky.

She walked up the front steps and cupped his face. Scott couldn't hear what she said, but Cory smiled and nodded in response. Then she turned and stepped right up to Scott, repeating what she'd done to Cory by cupping his face too. "You're pretty in a handsome way, but you're no flaming queen, sweetheart. Be good to my young friend."

Scott smiled and nodded, and she wandered back to her yard.

His gaze collided with Cory's, and all he wanted to do was rush forward and pull him into his arms and never let go.

"Say it again," Cory said.

Scott took a step forward. "I'm gay."

"No."

He took another step. "I'm full-on, big-flaming-queen gay."

Cory shook his head, and the next step brought Scott to the foot of the stairs. He took a breath and put every ounce of his heart into his next words. "I love you."

Cory launched off the porch and wrapped himself around Scott like a blanket. Arms and legs gripping tight enough to cut off circulation. Scott tightened his embrace, pulling Cory as close as humanly possible, and buried his face into the crook of Cory's neck. Then Cory started shaking.

"I'm so sorry, Core. I promise you I will do my best never to let you down again."

Cory pulled back, but he hadn't been crying; he was laughing. "I love you too, you big oaf." Then he dove in and kissed him, and just like that, the world righted itself again.

Epilogue

"Gillard, party of four," Scott said to the maître d', who slanted a long look of disdain down his nose at Scott and Cory. Surely it couldn't be because they were gay—it wasn't as if they had big neon signs over their heads. This restaurant was a favorite of Scott's father's; and it was in the heart of the gay district, so that couldn't be the reason for the sour perusal. Which meant it had to be—

"It's the hats," Cory whispered.

The hats?

Cal had told them there was a dress code and that sport jackets were mandatory. Scott had scoffed at the idea of a dress code to go for lunch, but he'd grabbed his leather coat, anyway. Of course, he and Cory were both in their best jeans, cowboy boots, shirts, and on-the-town hats. A couple of cowboys mixing it up with the GQ crowd.

He smiled.

"Right this way, sir," the maître d' said.

Scott and Cory followed, fingers brushing as they walked. That had been about the extent of Scott's PDA since officially announcing out loud that he was gay three months ago. Occasionally he pushed his boundaries, depending on where they were and what was happening. He'd gone as far as kiss Cory in public on the gay rodeo circuit, but on the regular circuit he still kept himself pretty much on the down low. But that was going to change.

The maître d' led them to a table near the windows overlooking San Francisco Bay. Scott's two dads stood to greet them. Without hesitation, Scott walked into his father's arms and welcomed a bone-crushing hug with one of his own, then another with Cal. He stepped back and smiled when Cory was swallowed up into their arms, but for nearly half their size, Cory gave back as good as he got. One of the many things he loved about him.

They'd become a family over the past few months, having made a point of regular lunches and dinners since they'd reconnected again. Many a long conversation with his father and Cal had helped him to overcome some lingering issues in accepting his true self. He would be forever grateful to have them in his life, and for Cory, who helped bring them all together. He was a little afraid to admit it, but things had been pretty great lately. Which was amazing, considering where he was two years ago, but so much of it was Cory. Never could Scott have imagined where he was now. Not only in love with another man, but one who burned so brilliantly.

Once they all settled in and placed their orders, Scott reached for Cory's hand. "I have something I want to share with all of you."

His father and Cal leaned forward, both pairs of eyes gleaming with expectation, and Cal fighting a smile.

"Easy, you two," Cory teased.

"A few months ago, I gave notice to my tenants to move out. At the end of the month, I'm moving back to my own ranch, and—" He looked over at Cory, who could barely contain spilling the beans. Who was he to keep any joy from his cowboy? "You tell them."

Cory's eyes lit up even brighter, which constantly amazed Scott. There always seemed to be yet another level of light to Cory. "Scott asked me to move in with him, and I said yes! Of course, I couldn't just burst that out before he even finished asking, so you know—" he waved his free hand in the air "—I had to make him work for it. Poor thing, but I could only let him grovel for so long because there was no way I was going to say no." Cory beamed up at him. "So come the first of next month, we'll be officially shacked up."

"Congratulations!" Scott's dads said together.

"This calls for a proper toast," Cal said, turning to flag a waiter over.

"I'm really happy for you, Scott," his father said. He reached across the table, taking Scott's hand and giving it a squeeze. "And you too, Cory."

"Thank you." Cory leaned into him.

"I have a little more news to share," Scott said. Everyone paused, giving him their full attention. He hadn't told Cory about his plans yet but thought today would be the perfect time for his announcement. "I've decided to return to the PBR. Full-time. And . . . I'm going to ride openly gay."

"Scott . . ." Cory's voice was barely above a whisper, but the awe and admiration in it was clear as a bell. "Are you sure?"

"One hundred and ten percent." Scott smiled, and Cory threw his arms around Scott's neck. He kissed his cheek and then in his ear said, "My cowboy. I love you."

"I only have a few good years or so left at competition level," Scott continued when Cory sat back in his chair, "but I'm going to do Tripp's work from the chutes, like he should have been able to before his career got taken away from him."

"That's fantastic news," Cal said. "We really need a bottle of champagne now."

"I am so proud of you, son."

"Thank you, Dad." Scott looked down at his glass for a second. "I'm just so glad I'm able to share this with you. That you're here. You and Cal." He turned to Cory. "And I couldn't have done any of this without you."

Cory reached out and traced Scott's mouth with a fingertip. "I love this smile."

Scott stilled his hand and kissed his fingers. "I love you."

"Champagne!" Cal announced and began pouring a round of bubbly. They held their glasses up, meeting over the center of the table, and his dad said, "To family, to love, and to cowboys."

Bubbles tickled his nose as he drank, then he put his glass down, pulled Cory into his arms, and kissed him, right there in the middle of the restaurant for all to see. And he didn't care. It had taken a long time, a lot of dark days, but he got here, and he couldn't imagine anywhere better.

Read the Pickup Men series from the beginning:

ISBN: 978-1-62649-057-4

ISBN: 978-1-62649-148-9

Dear Reader,

Thank you for reading L.C. Chase's *Pulling Leather*!

We know your time is precious and you have many, many entertainment options, so it means a lot that you've chosen to spend your time reading. We really hope you enjoyed it.

We'd be honored if you'd consider posting a review—good or bad—on sites like **Amazon, Barnes & Noble, Kobo, Goodreads, Twitter, Facebook, Tumblr,** and your blog or website. We'd also be honored if you told your friends and family about this book. Word of mouth is a book's lifeblood!

For more information on upcoming releases, author interviews, blog tours, contests, giveaways, and more, please sign up for our weekly, spam-free newsletter and visit us around the web:

Newsletter: tinyurl.com/RiptideSignup
Twitter: twitter.com/RiptideBooks
Facebook: facebook.com/RiptidePublishing
Goodreads: tinyurl.com/RiptideOnGoodreads
Tumblr: riptidepublishing.tumblr.com

Thank you so much for Reading the Rainbow!

RiptidePublishing.com

ALSO BY
L.C. CHASE

Pickup Men series

Pickup Men

Let It Ride

Love Brokers: Mister Romance

Riding with Heaven

Long Tall Drink

ABOUT THE AUTHOR

Cover artist by day, author by night, L.C. Chase is a hopeless romantic and adventure seeker. After a decade of traveling three continents, she now calls the Canadian West Coast home. When not writing sensual tales of beautiful men falling in love, she can be found designing book covers with said beautiful men, drawing, horseback riding, or hiking the trails with her goofy four-legged roommate.

L.C. is a 2014 Lambda Literary Award Finalist for *Pickup Men*; a 2013 EPIC eBook Awards Finalist for *Long Tall Drink*; and a 2013-2014 Ariana eBook Cover Art Awards Finalist. She also won an honorable mention in the 2012 Rainbow Awards for *Riding with Heaven*.

You can visit L.C. at www.lcchase.com.

CPSIA information can be obtained
at www.ICGtesting.com
Printed in the USA
LVOW12s1543180218
567038LV00002B/455/P